EDGAR ALLAN POE'S

THE NARRATIVE OF
ARTHUR GORDON
PYM

A GRAPHIC NOVEL

BY MANUEL MORINI &
ENRIQUE ALCATENA

STONE ARCH BOOKS
A CAPSTONE IMPRINT

Graphic Revolve is published by Stone Arch Books,
1710 Roe Crest Drive, North Mankato, Minnesota, 56003
www.mycapstone.com

Cataloging-in-Publication Data is available on the
Library of Congress website.
ISBN 978-1-4965-5576-2 (library binding)
ISBN 978-1-4965-5582-3 (paperback)
ISBN 978-1-4965-5588-5 (eBook PDF)

Summary: A young man gets caught up in a whirlwind
adventure at sea.

By Manuel Morini & Enrique Alcatena

Translated into the English language by
Trusted Translations.

Printed in the United States of America.
010370F17

TABLE OF CONTENTS

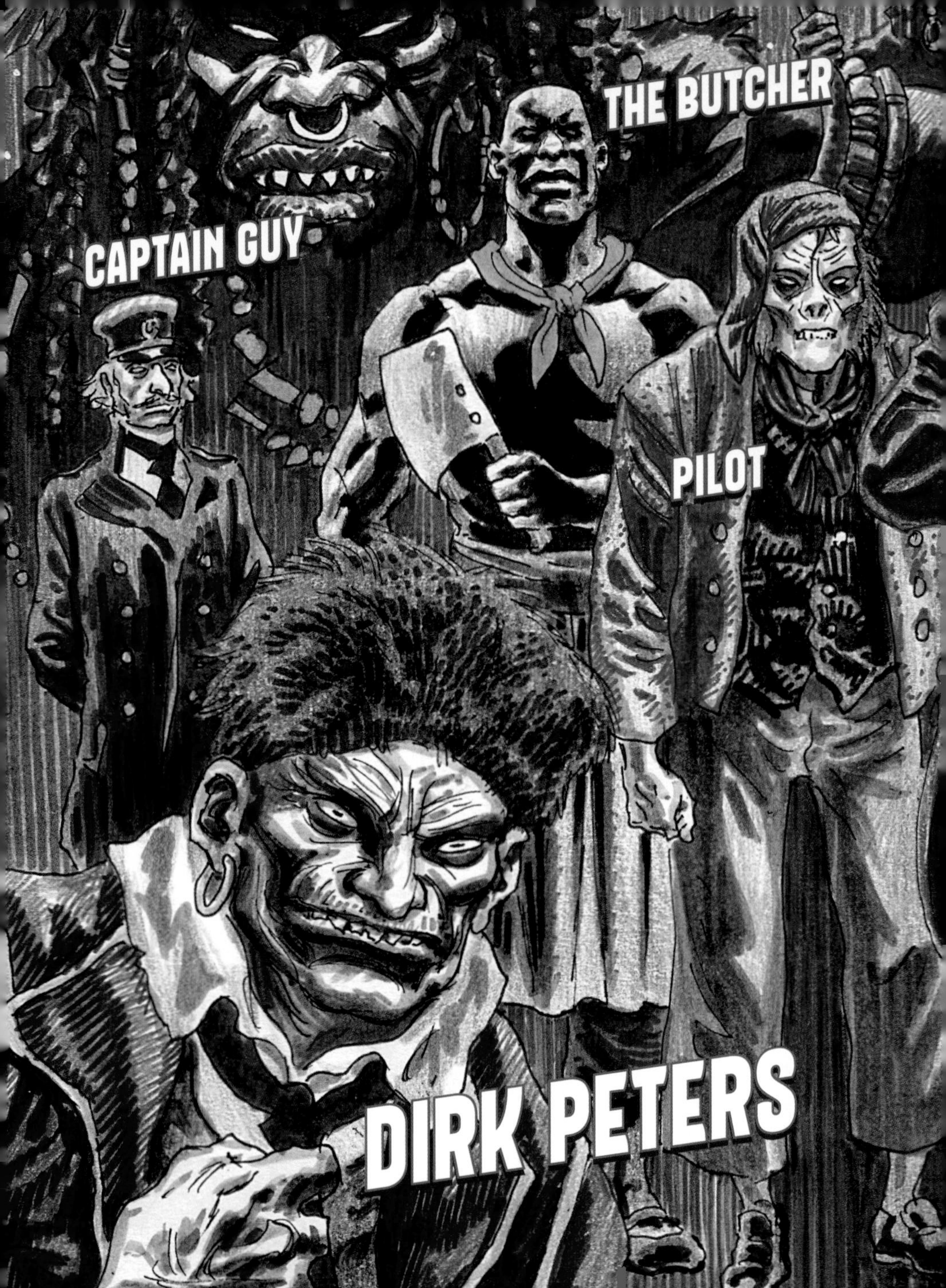
THE BUTCHER
CAPTAIN GUY
PILOT
DIRK PETERS

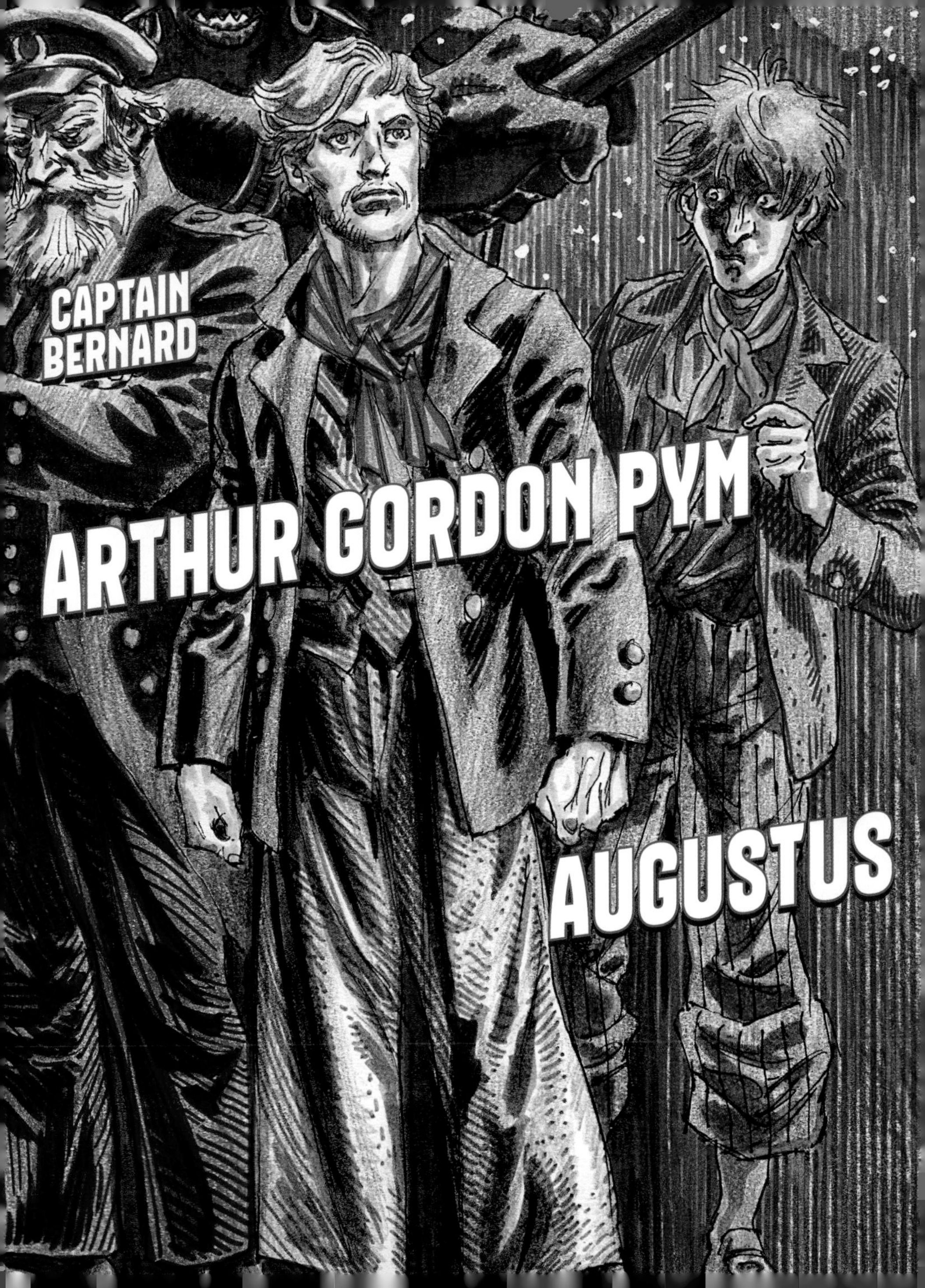
CAPTAIN BERNARD
ARTHUR GORDON PYM
AUGUSTUS

CHAPTER 1
THE STOWAWAY

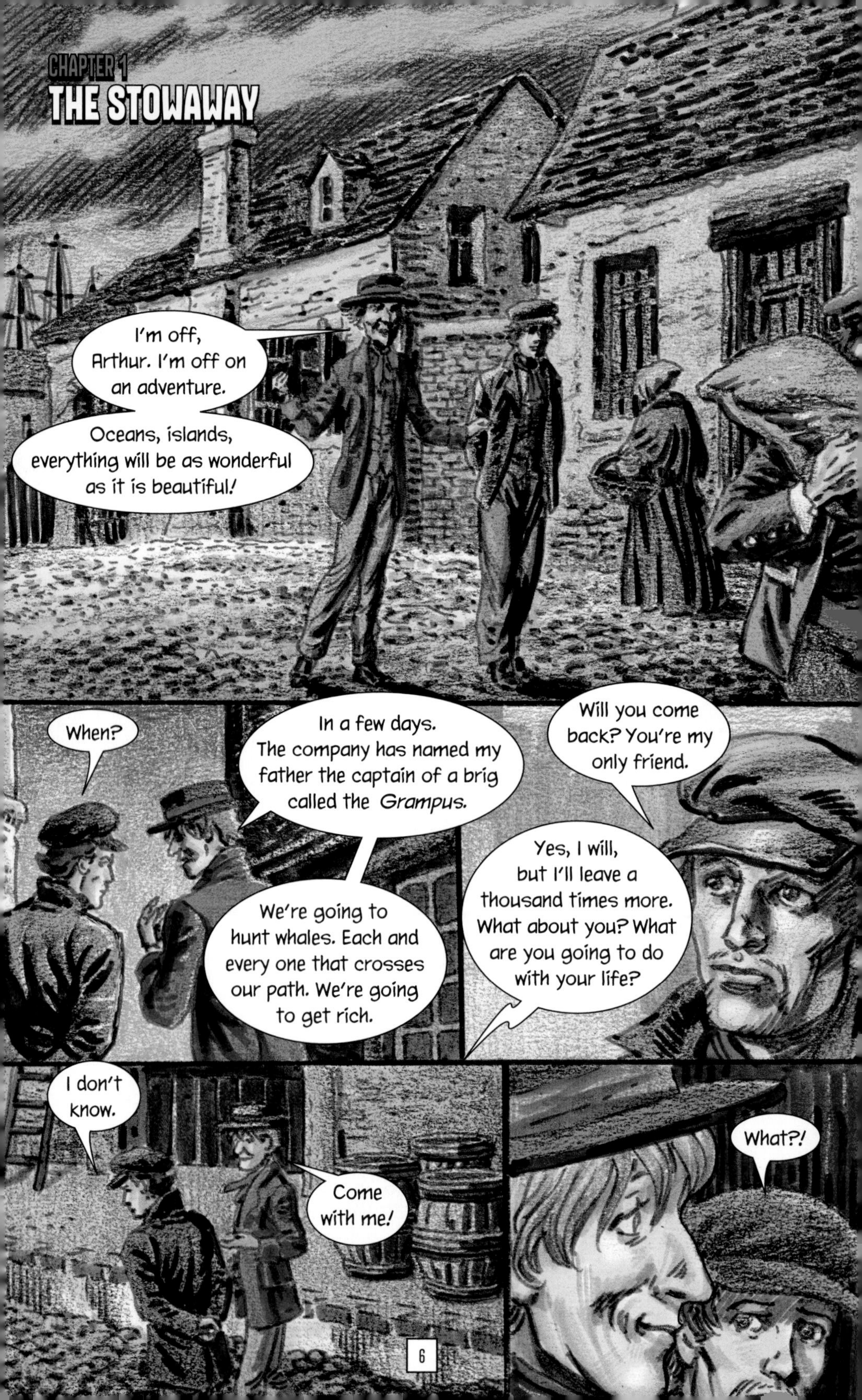
I'm off, Arthur. I'm off on an adventure.
Oceans, islands, everything will be as wonderful as it is beautiful!
When?
In a few days. The company has named my father the captain of a brig called the *Grampus*.
We're going to hunt whales. Each and every one that crosses our path. We're going to get rich.
Will you come back? You're my only friend.
Yes, I will, but I'll leave a thousand times more. What about you? What are you going to do with your life?
I don't know.
Come with me!
What?!

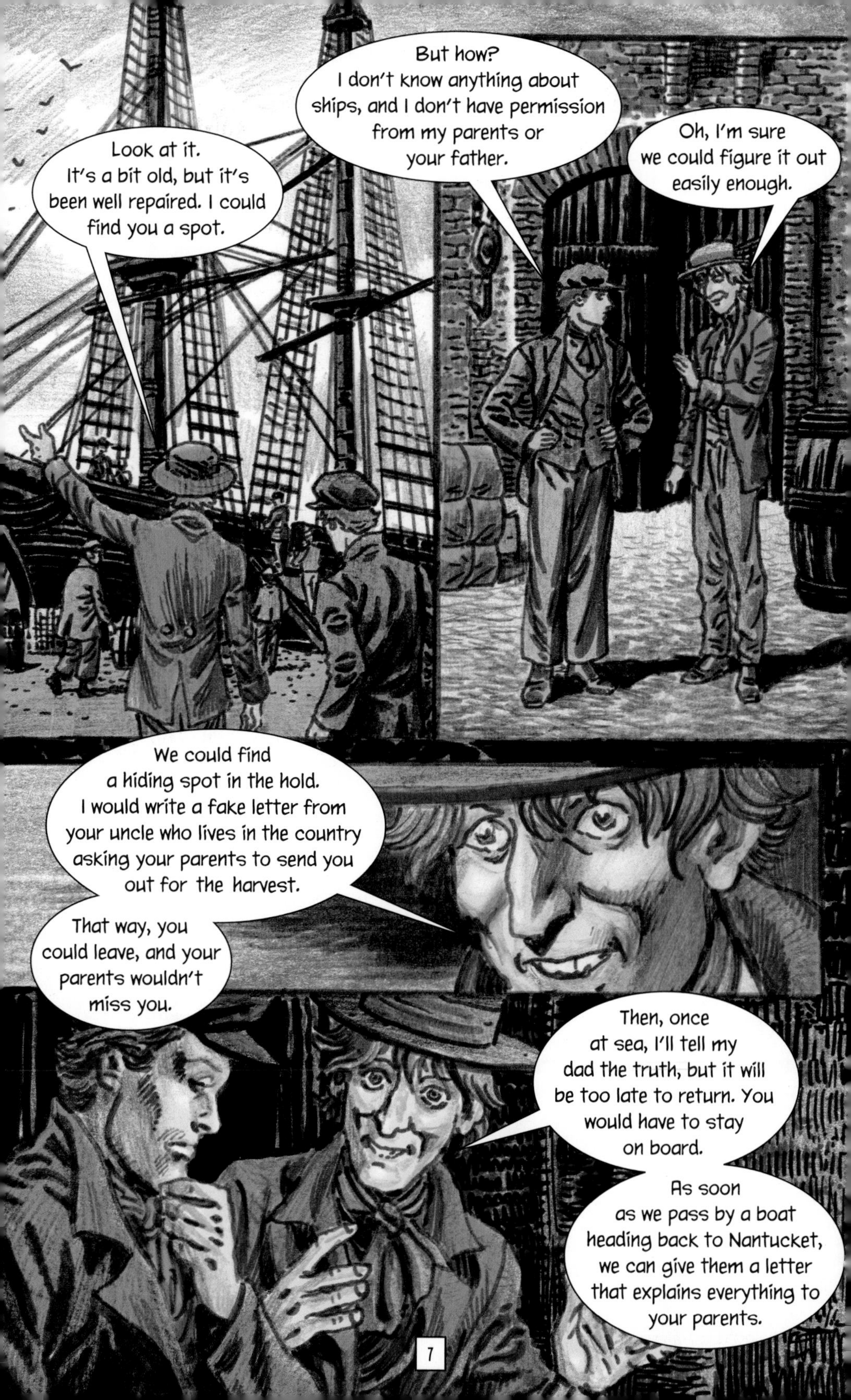
Look at it. It's a bit old, but it's been well repaired. I could find you a spot.
But how? I don't know anything about ships, and I don't have permission from my parents or your father.
Oh, I'm sure we could figure it out easily enough.
We could find a hiding spot in the hold. I would write a fake letter from your uncle who lives in the country asking your parents to send you out for the harvest.
That way, you could leave, and your parents wouldn't miss you.
Then, once at sea, I'll tell my dad the truth, but it will be too late to return. You would have to stay on board.
As soon as we pass by a boat heading back to Nantucket, we can give them a letter that explains everything to your parents.

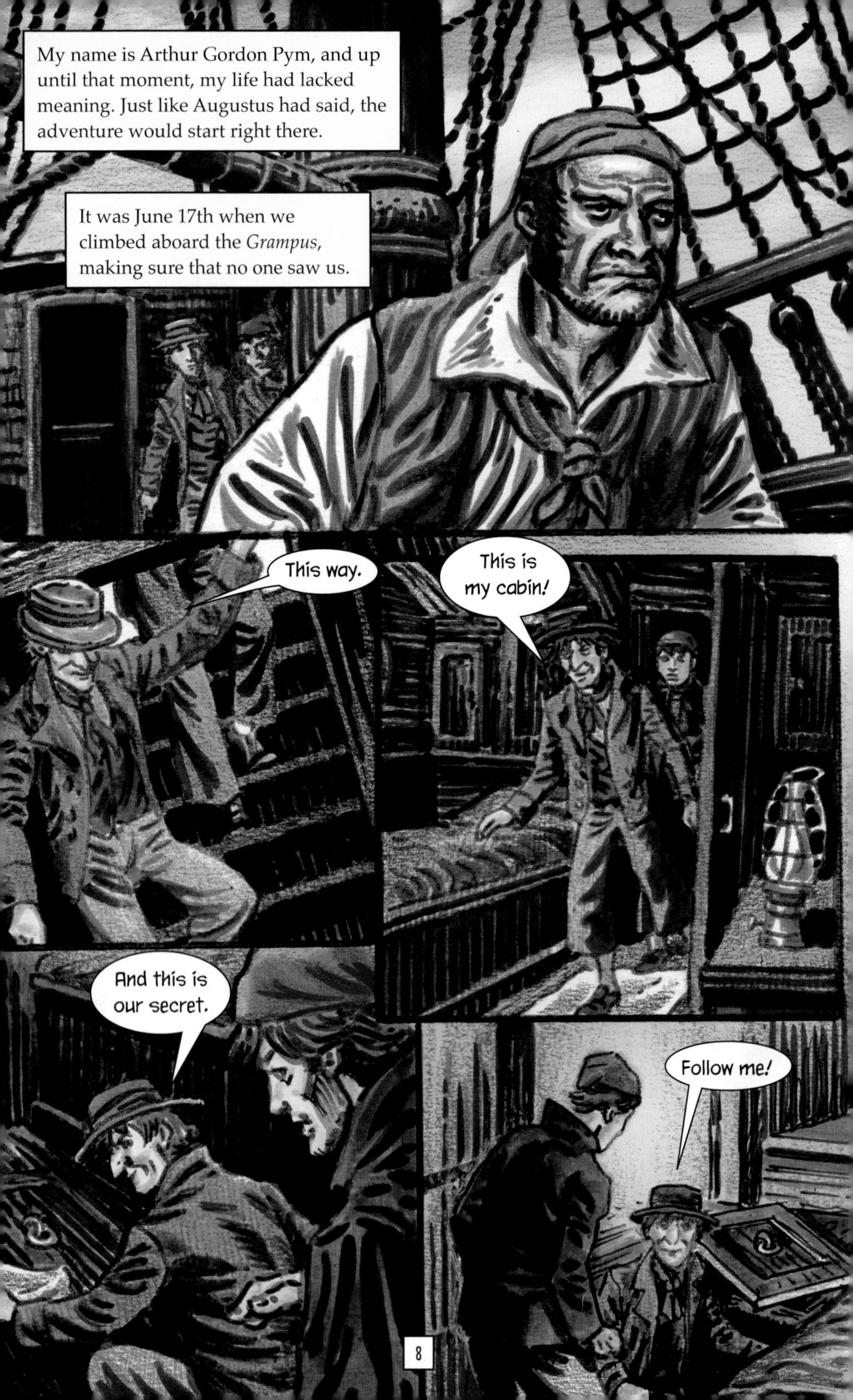

My name is Arthur Gordon Pym, and up until that moment, my life had lacked meaning. Just like Augustus had said, the adventure would start right there.
It was June 17th when we climbed aboard the *Grampus*, making sure that no one saw us.
This way.
This is my cabin!
And this is our secret.
Follow me!

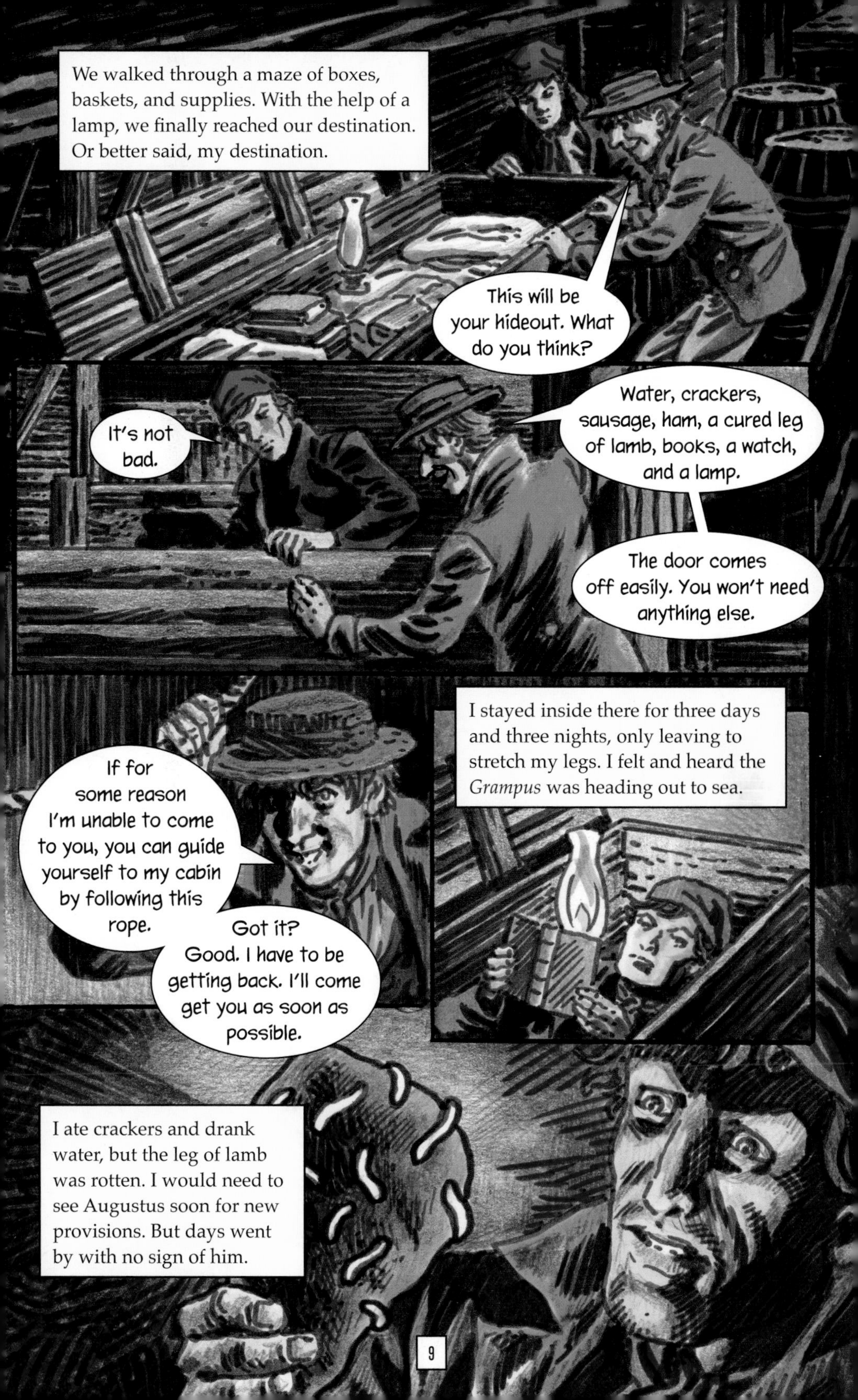
We walked through a maze of boxes, baskets, and supplies. With the help of a lamp, we finally reached our destination. Or better said, my destination.
This will be your hideout. What do you think?
It's not bad.
Water, crackers, sausage, ham, a cured leg of lamb, books, a watch, and a lamp.
The door comes off easily. You won't need anything else.
If for some reason I'm unable to come to you, you can guide yourself to my cabin by following this rope.
Got it? Good. I have to be getting back. I'll come get you as soon as possible.
I stayed inside there for three days and three nights, only leaving to stretch my legs. I felt and heard the *Grampus* was heading out to sea.
I ate crackers and drank water, but the leg of lamb was rotten. I would need to see Augustus soon for new provisions. But days went by with no sign of him.

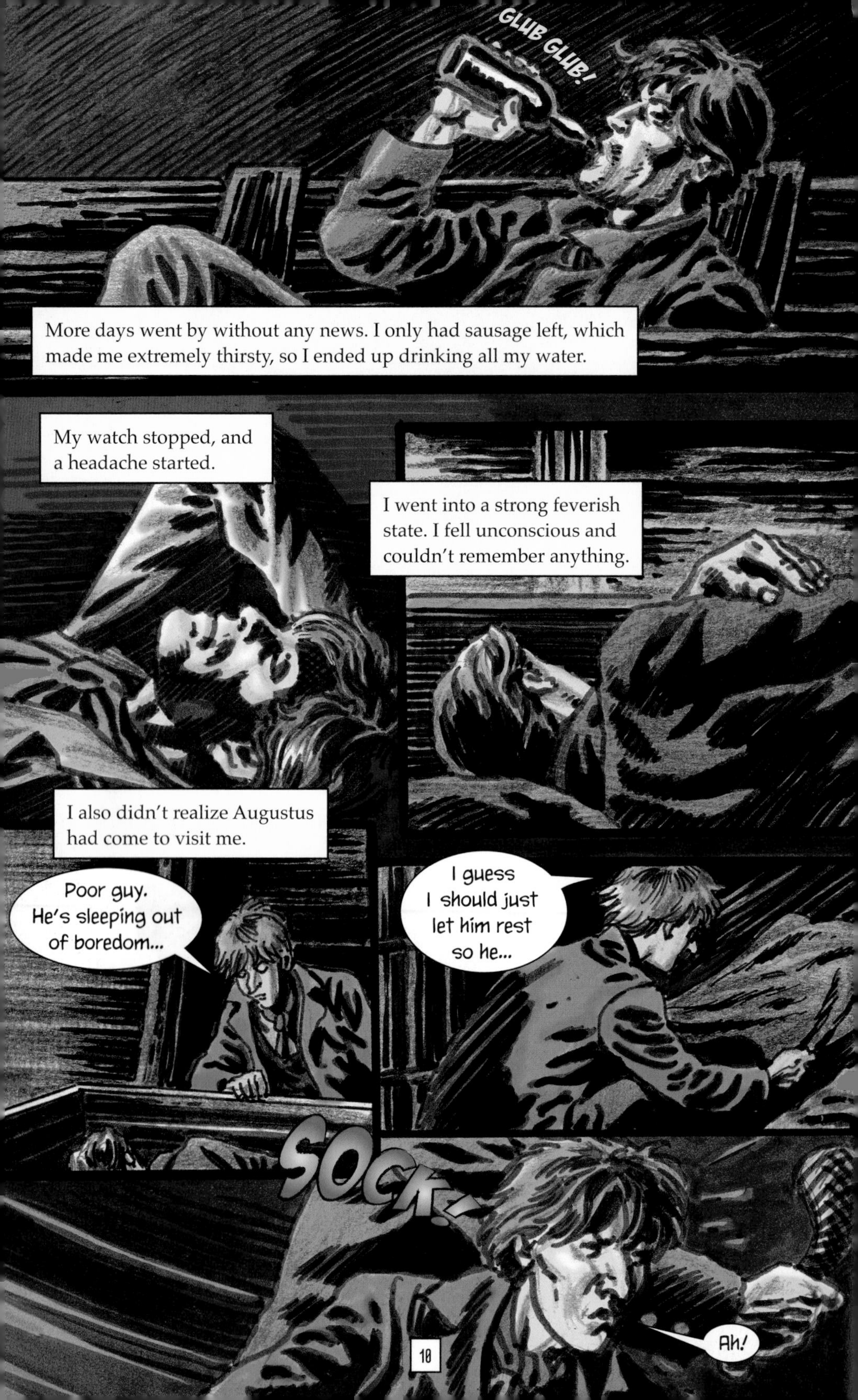
GLUB GLUB!
More days went by without any news. I only had sausage left, which made me extremely thirsty, so I ended up drinking all my water.
My watch stopped, and a headache started.
I went into a strong feverish state. I fell unconscious and couldn't remember anything.
I also didn't realize Augustus had come to visit me.
Poor guy. He's sleeping out of boredom...
I guess I should just let him rest so he...
SOCK!
Ah!

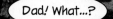

Dad! What...?

Calm down, boy. We've just taken hold of the *Grampus*, and your father refused to obey me. That's all.

And now, get walking. To the deck. This cabin doesn't belong to you anymore.

This is all I could find, for now. We have to keep looking.

How many prisoners are there?

Twenty-two men in the hold.

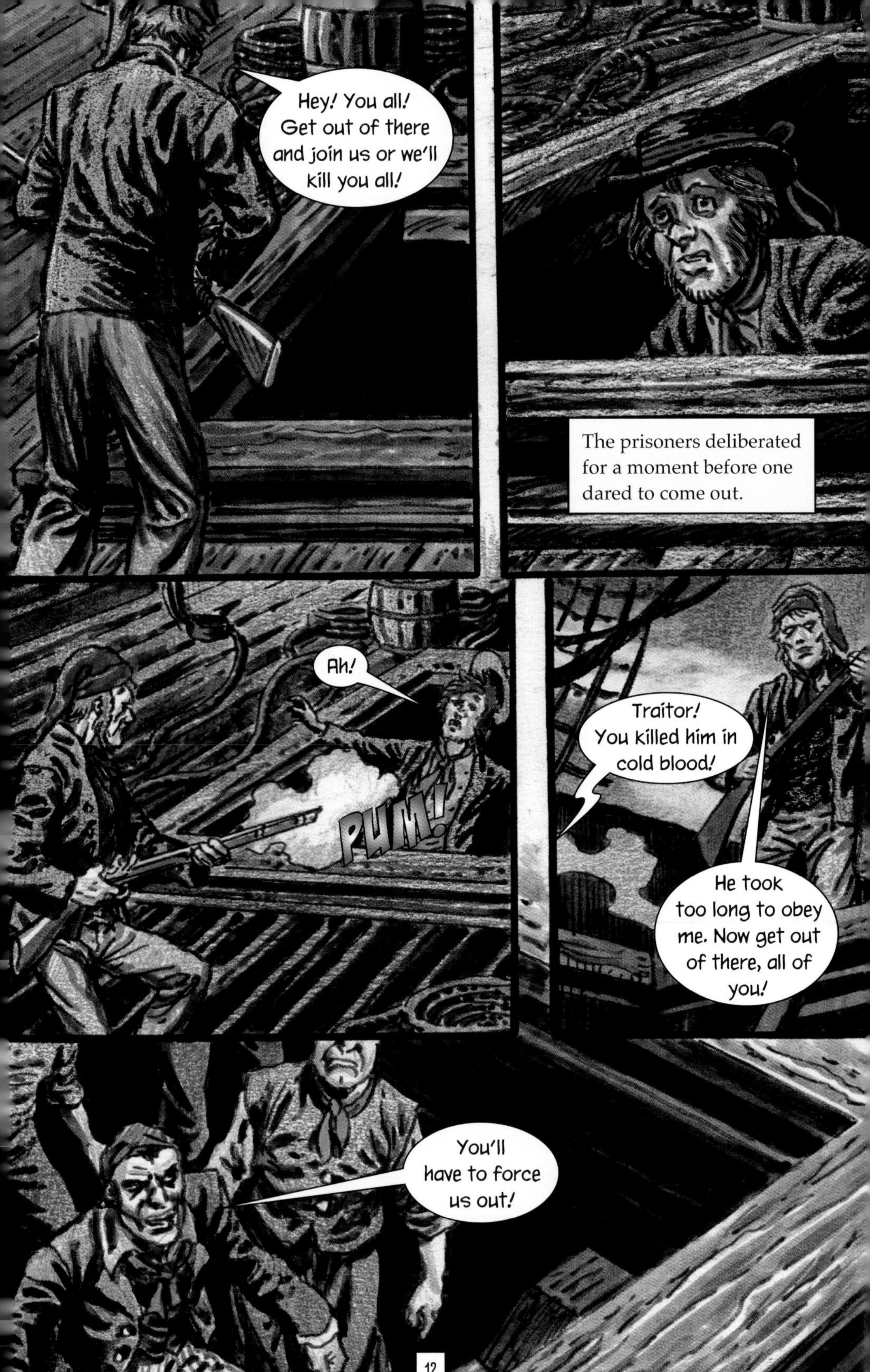
Hey! You all! Get out of there and join us or we'll kill you all!
The prisoners deliberated for a moment before one dared to come out.
Ah!
PUM!
Traitor! You killed him in cold blood!
He took too long to obey me. Now get out of there, all of you!
You'll have to force us out!

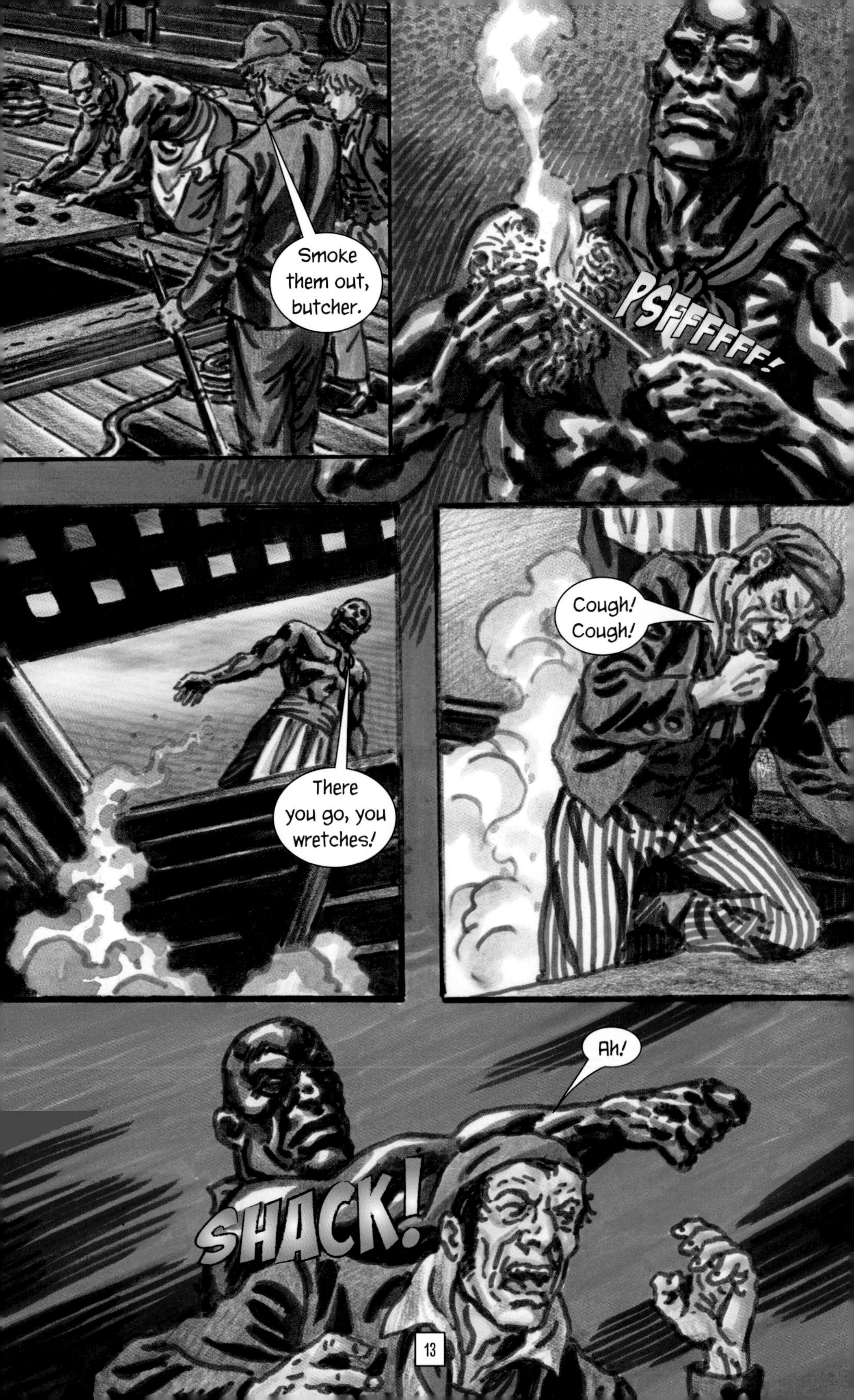
Smoke them out, butcher.
PSFFFFFFF!
There you go, you wretches!
Cough! Cough!
Ah!
SHACK!

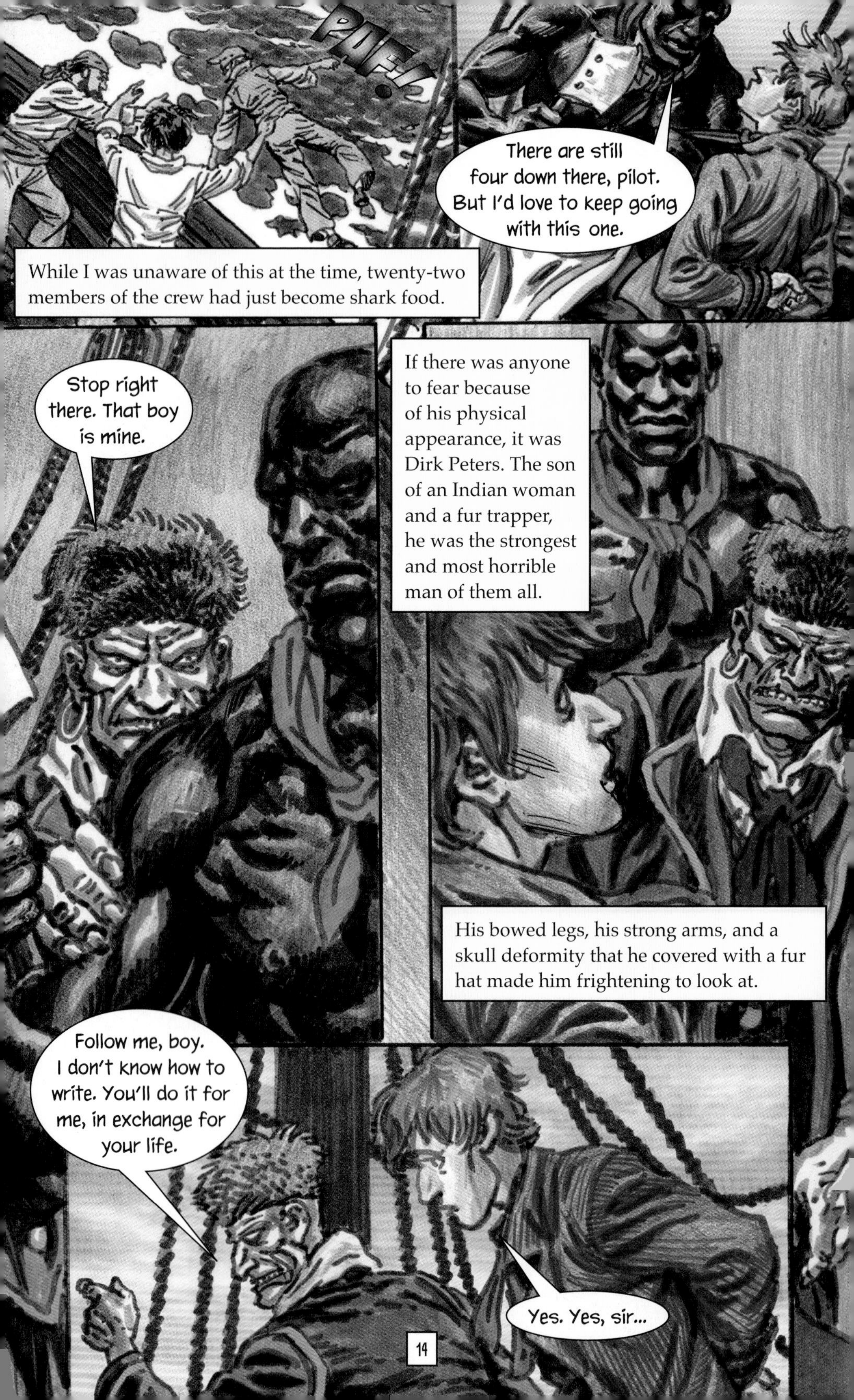
PUF!
There are still four down there, pilot. But I'd love to keep going with this one.
While I was unaware of this at the time, twenty-two members of the crew had just become shark food.
Stop right there. That boy is mine.
If there was anyone to fear because of his physical appearance, it was Dirk Peters. The son of an Indian woman and a fur trapper, he was the strongest and most horrible man of them all.
His bowed legs, his strong arms, and a skull deformity that he covered with a fur hat made him frightening to look at.
Follow me, boy. I don't know how to write. You'll do it for me, in exchange for your life.
Yes. Yes, sir...

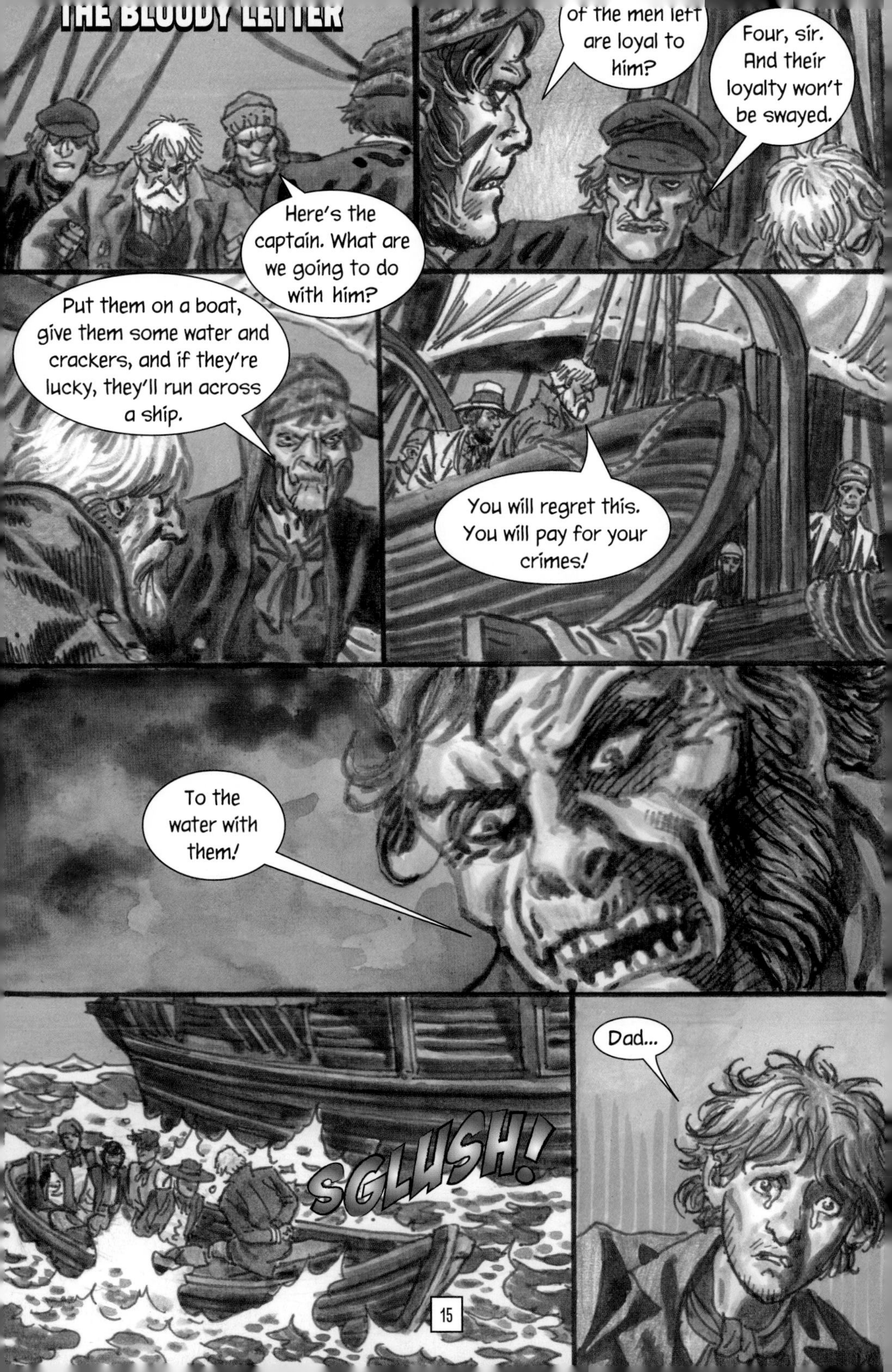
of the men left are loyal to him?
Four, sir. And their loyalty won't be swayed.
Here's the captain. What are we going to do with him?
Put them on a boat, give them some water and crackers, and if they're lucky, they'll run across a ship.
You will regret this. You will pay for your crimes!
To the water with them!
SGLUSH!
Dad...

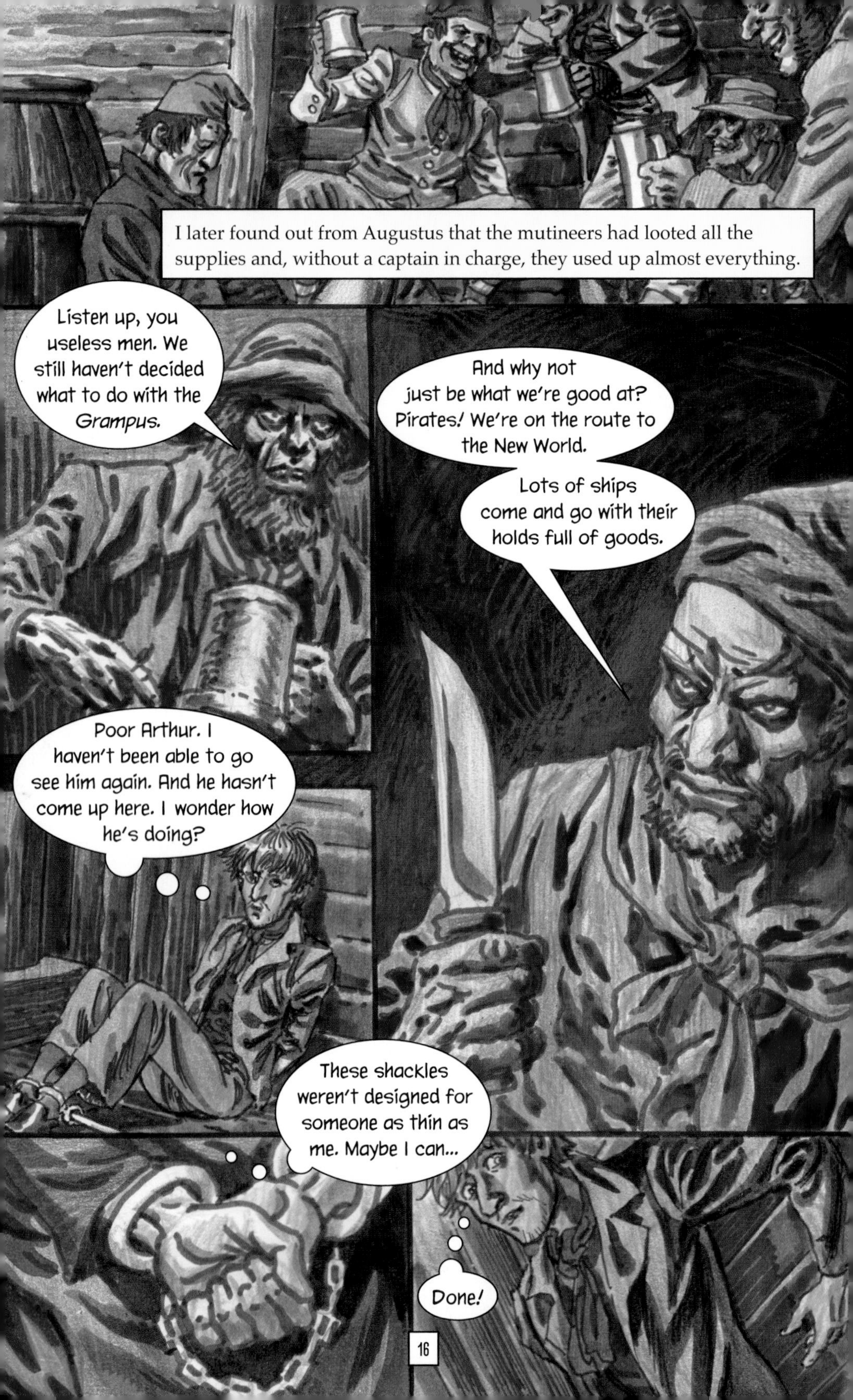
I later found out from Augustus that the mutineers had looted all the supplies and, without a captain in charge, they used up almost everything.
Listen up, you useless men. We still haven't decided what to do with the *Grampus*.
And why not just be what we're good at? Pirates! We're on the route to the New World.
Lots of ships come and go with their holds full of goods.
Poor Arthur. I haven't been able to go see him again. And he hasn't come up here. I wonder how he's doing?
These shackles weren't designed for someone as thin as me. Maybe I can...
Done!

I know that Augustus wanted to help me, but at that moment, help was impossible.

I have to let him know somehow. I have paper, but that's it.

I've got it!

And that's how Augustus got his ink.

I hope he finds my letter.

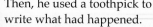

Then, he used a toothpick to write what had happened.

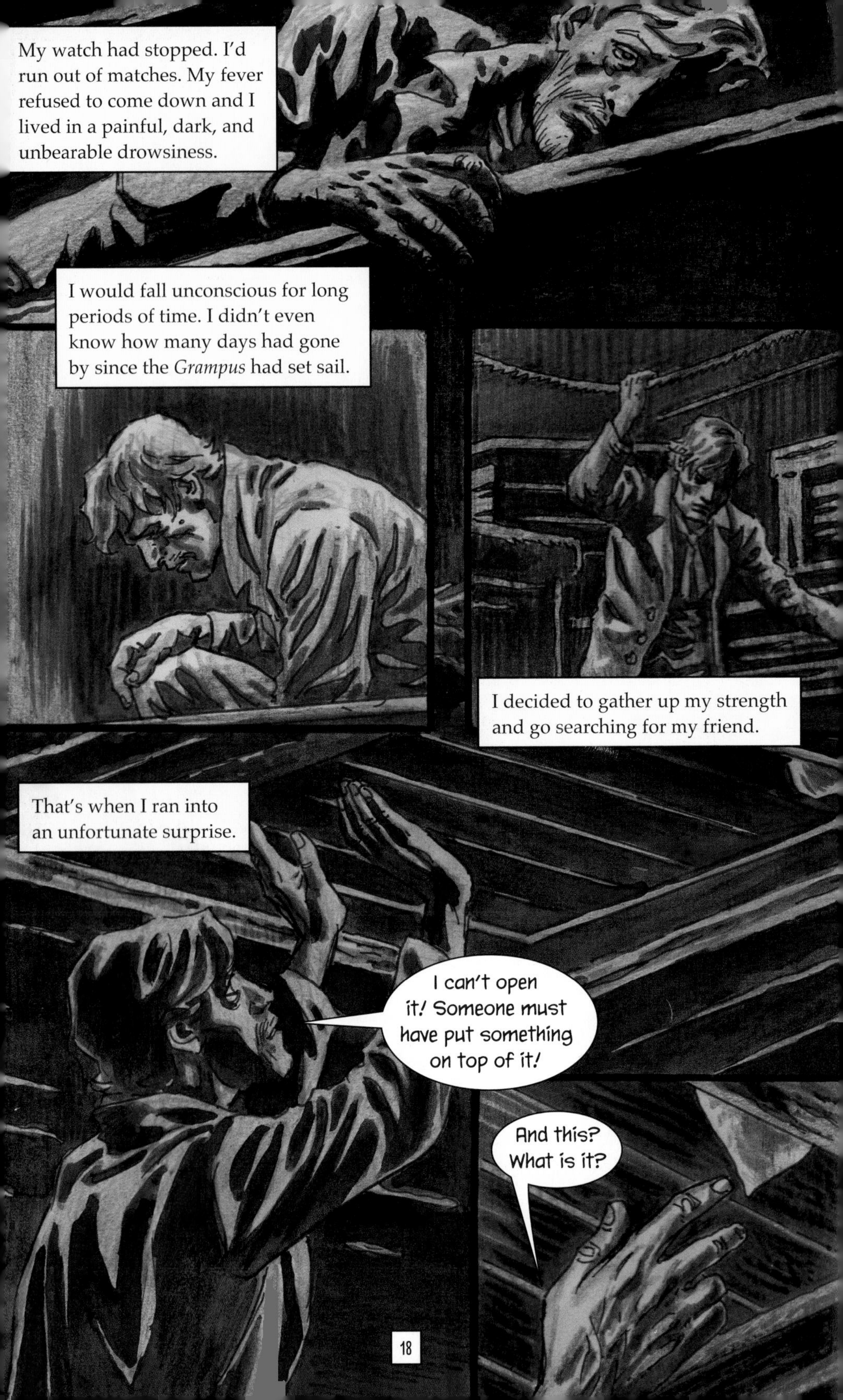
My watch had stopped. I'd run out of matches. My fever refused to come down and I lived in a painful, dark, and unbearable drowsiness.
I would fall unconscious for long periods of time. I didn't even know how many days had gone by since the *Grampus* had set sail.
I decided to gather up my strength and go searching for my friend.
That's when I ran into an unfortunate surprise.
I can't open it! Someone must have put something on top of it!
And this? What is it?

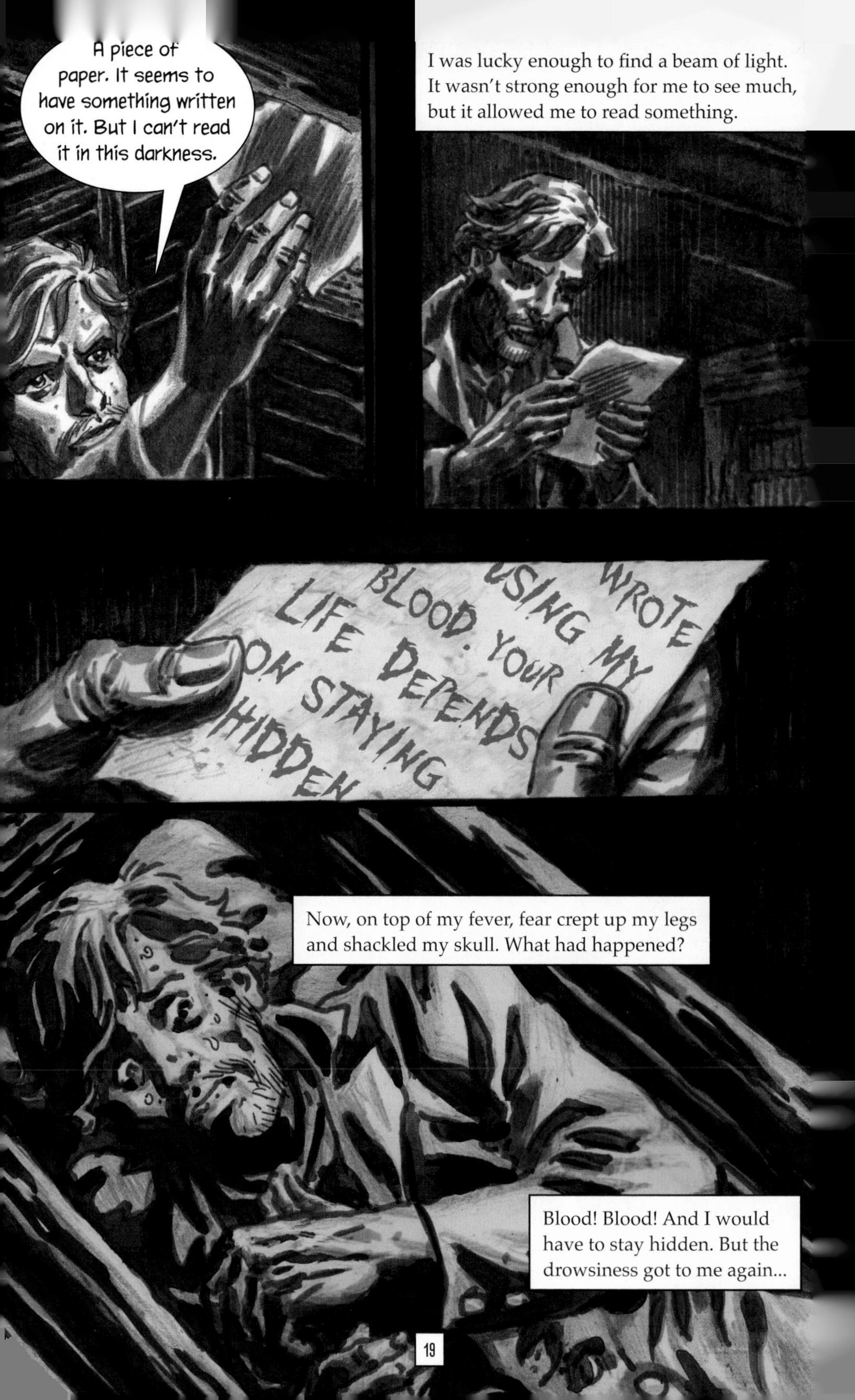
A piece of paper. It seems to have something written on it. But I can't read it in this darkness.
I was lucky enough to find a beam of light. It wasn't strong enough for me to see much, but it allowed me to read something.
WROTE USING MY BLOOD. YOUR LIFE DEPENDS ON STAYING HIDDEN
Now, on top of my fever, fear crept up my legs and shackled my skull. What had happened?
Blood! Blood! And I would have to stay hidden. But the drowsiness got to me again...

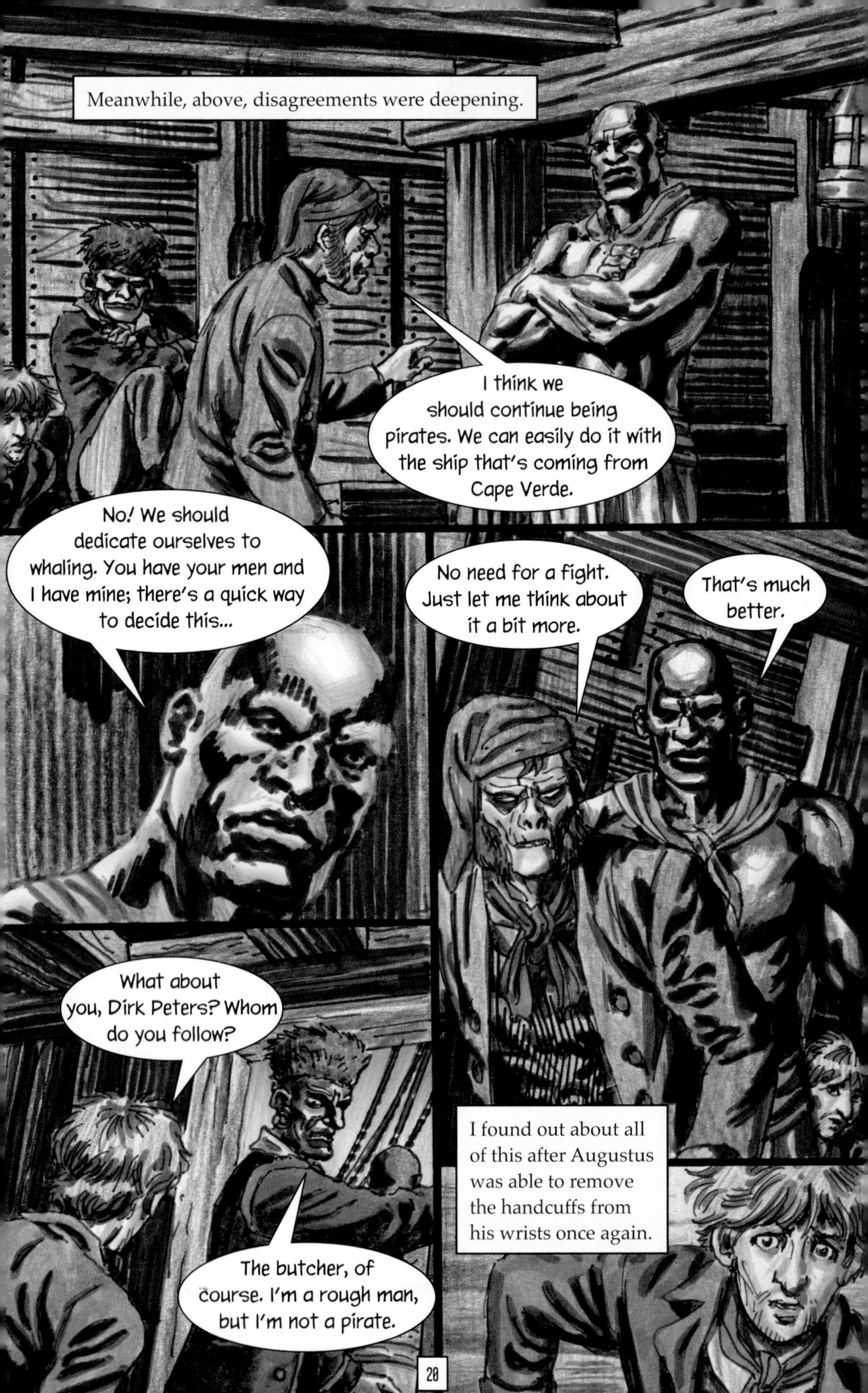
Meanwhile, above, disagreements were deepening.
I think we should continue being pirates. We can easily do it with the ship that's coming from Cape Verde.
No! We should dedicate ourselves to whaling. You have your men and I have mine; there's a quick way to decide this...
No need for a fight. Just let me think about it a bit more.
That's much better.
What about you, Dirk Peters? Whom do you follow?
The butcher, of course. I'm a rough man, but I'm not a pirate.
I found out about all of this after Augustus was able to remove the handcuffs from his wrists once again.

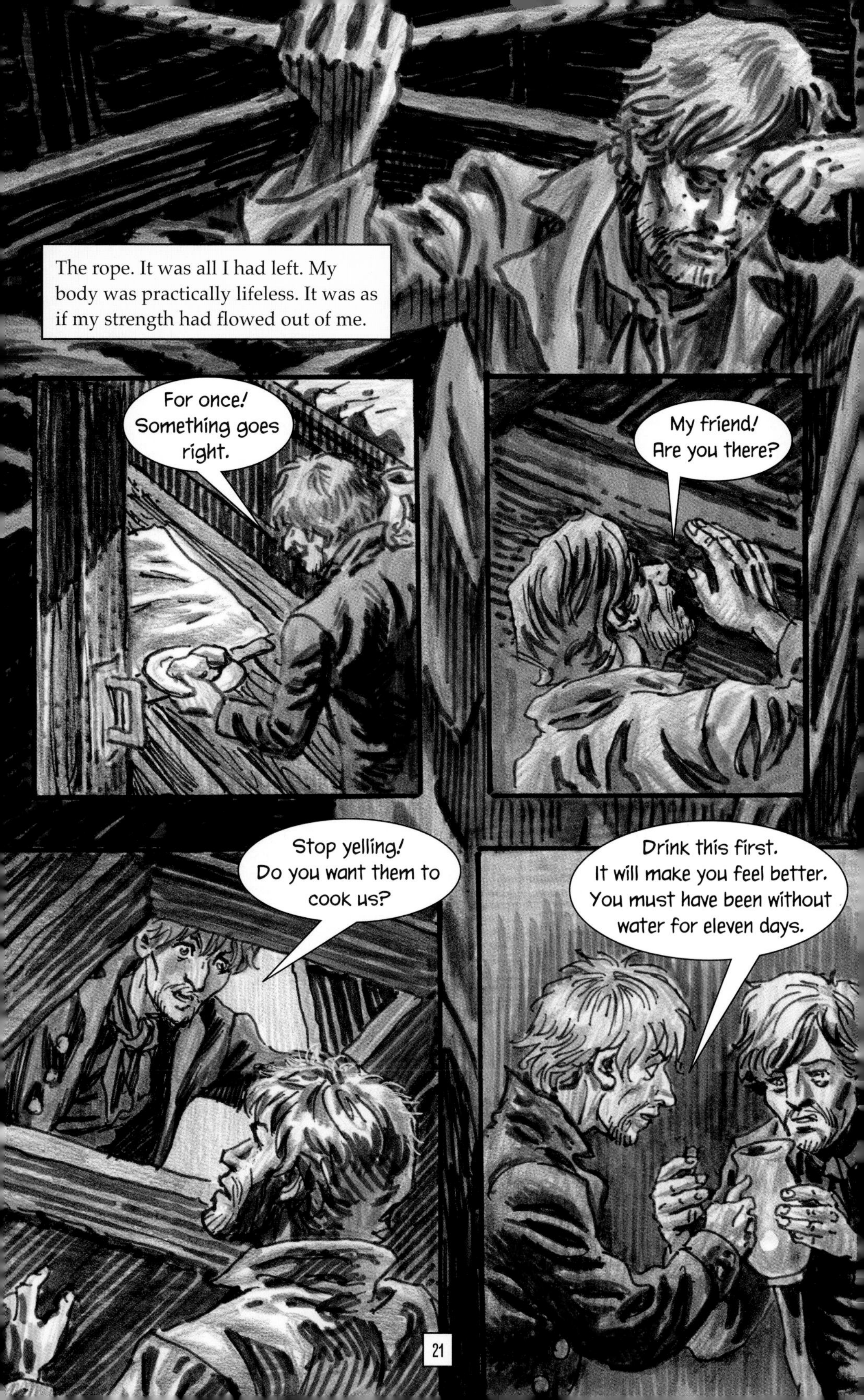
The rope. It was all I had left. My body was practically lifeless. It was as if my strength had flowed out of me.
For once! Something goes right.
My friend! Are you there?
Stop yelling! Do you want them to cook us?
Drink this first. It will make you feel better. You must have been without water for eleven days.

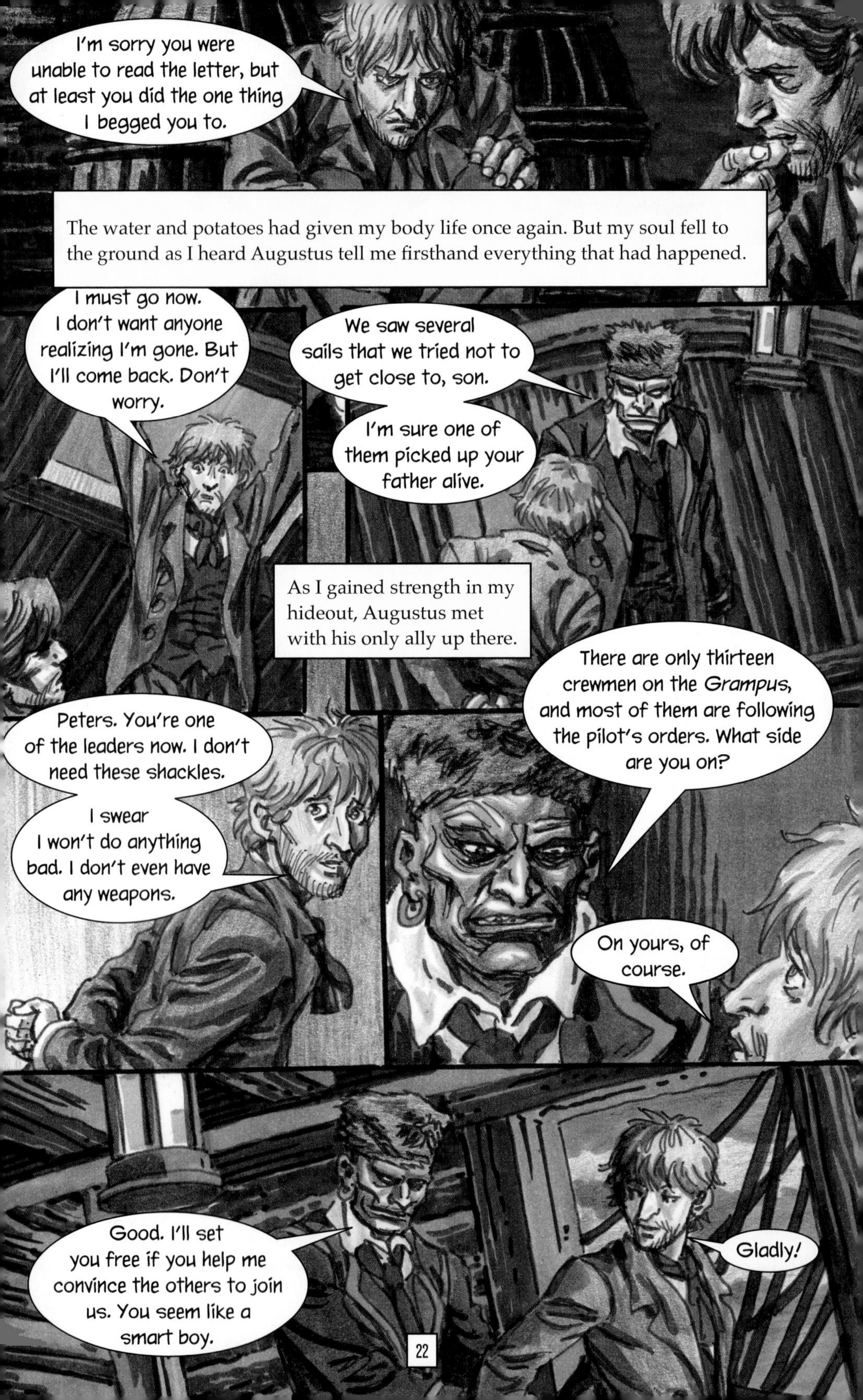
I'm sorry you were unable to read the letter, but at least you did the one thing I begged you to.
The water and potatoes had given my body life once again. But my soul fell to the ground as I heard Augustus tell me firsthand everything that had happened.
I must go now. I don't want anyone realizing I'm gone. But I'll come back. Don't worry.
We saw several sails that we tried not to get close to, son.
I'm sure one of them picked up your father alive.
As I gained strength in my hideout, Augustus met with his only ally up there.
Peters. You're one of the leaders now. I don't need these shackles.
I swear I won't do anything bad. I don't even have any weapons.
There are only thirteen crewmen on the *Grampus*, and most of them are following the pilot's orders. What side are you on?
On yours, of course.
Good. I'll set you free if you help me convince the others to join us. You seem like a smart boy.
Gladly!

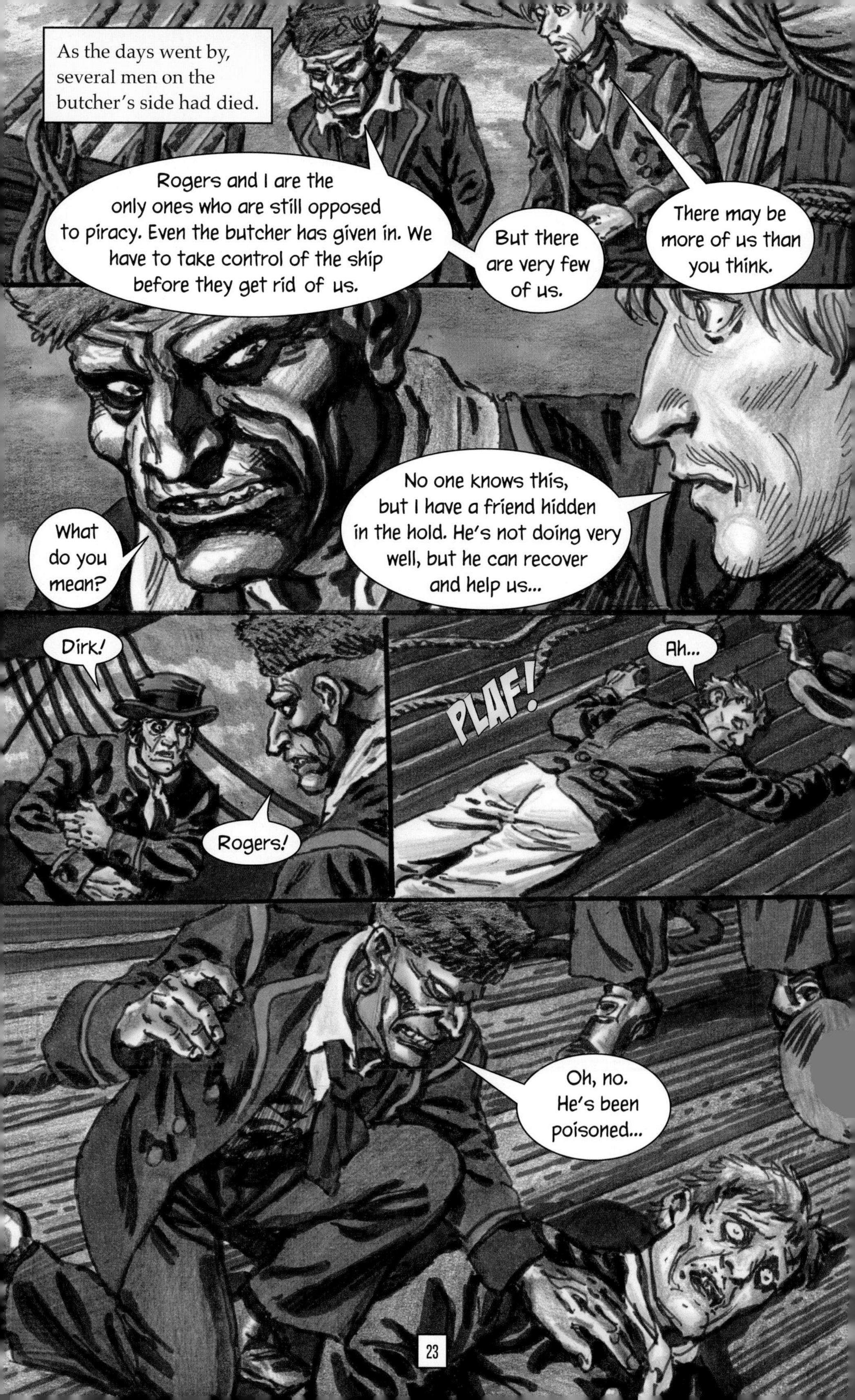
As the days went by, several men on the butcher's side had died.
Rogers and I are the only ones who are still opposed to piracy. Even the butcher has given in. We have to take control of the ship before they get rid of us.
But there are very few of us.
There may be more of us than you think.
What do you mean?
No one knows this, but I have a friend hidden in the hold. He's not doing very well, but he can recover and help us...
Dirk!
Rogers!
PLAF!
Ah...
Oh, no. He's been poisoned...

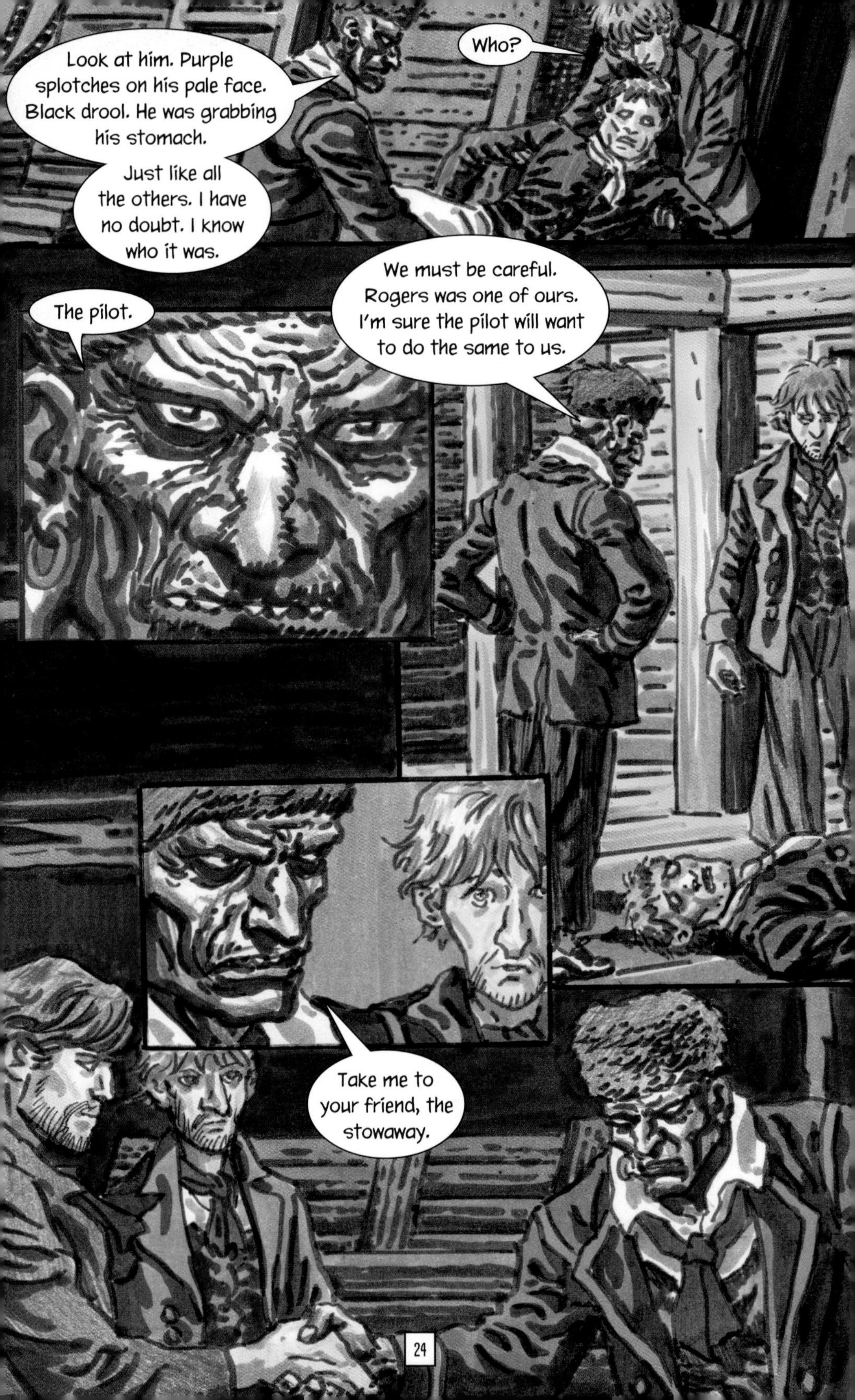
Look at him. Purple splotches on his pale face. Black drool. He was grabbing his stomach.
Who?
Just like all the others. I have no doubt. I know who it was.
The pilot.
We must be careful. Rogers was one of ours. I'm sure the pilot will want to do the same to us.
Take me to your friend, the stowaway.

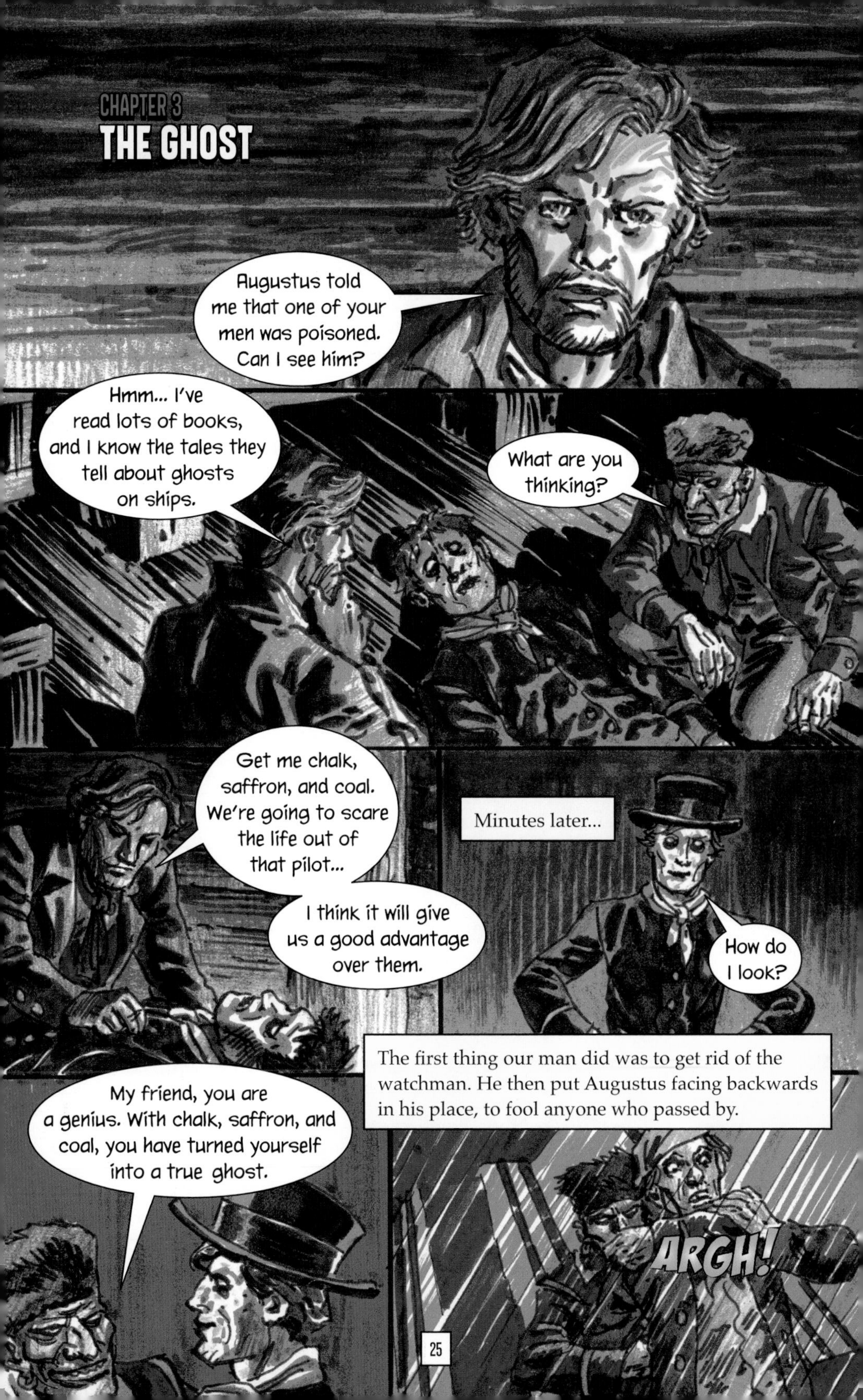
CHAPTER 3
THE GHOST
Augustus told me that one of your men was poisoned. Can I see him?
Hmm... I've read lots of books, and I know the tales they tell about ghosts on ships.
What are you thinking?
Get me chalk, saffron, and coal. We're going to scare the life out of that pilot...
I think it will give us a good advantage over them.
Minutes later...
How do I look?
My friend, you are a genius. With chalk, saffron, and coal, you have turned yourself into a true ghost.
The first thing our man did was to get rid of the watchman. He then put Augustus facing backwards in his place, to fool anyone who passed by.
ARGH!

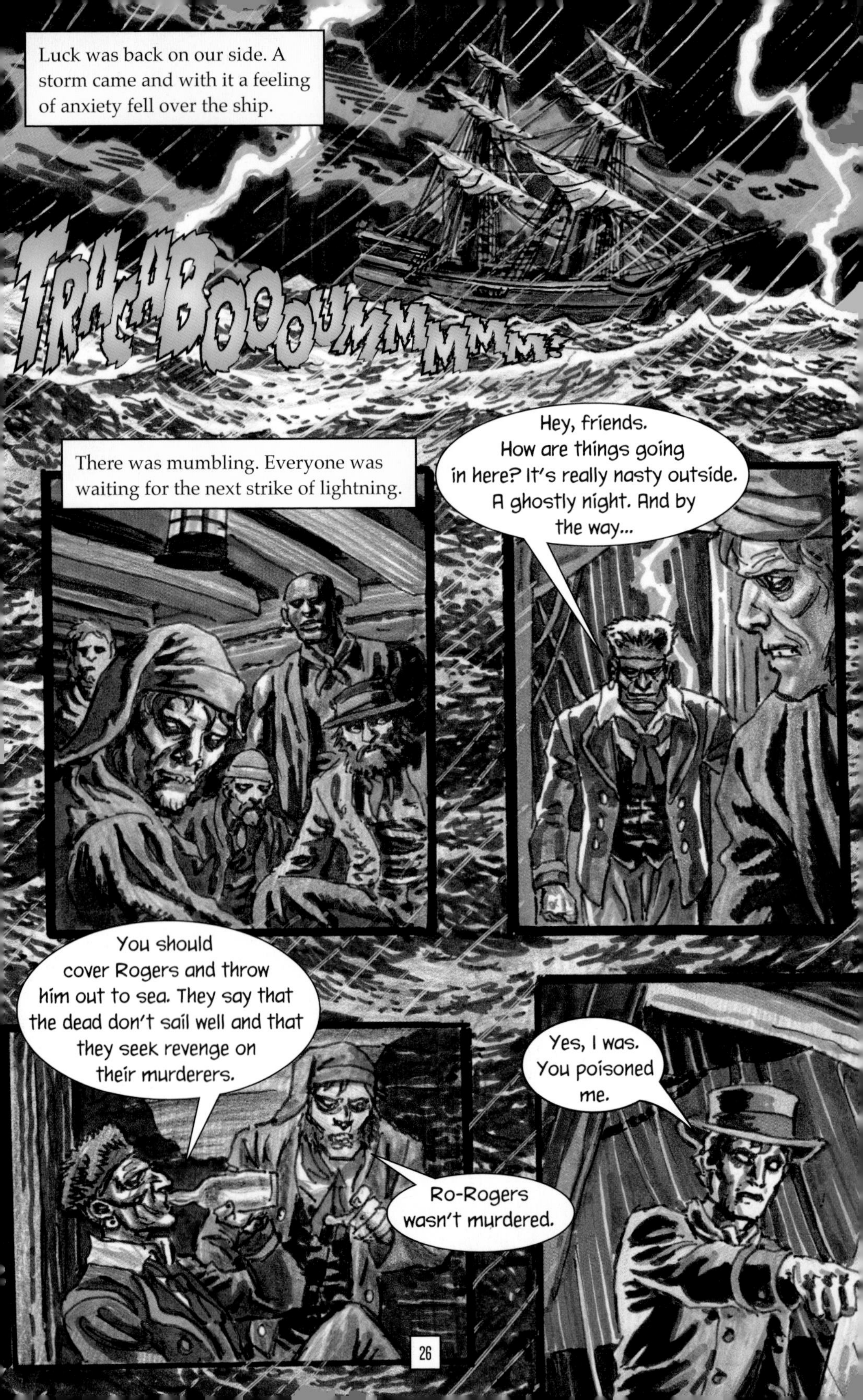
Luck was back on our side. A storm came and with it a feeling of anxiety fell over the ship.
TRACABOOOUMMMMM!
There was mumbling. Everyone was waiting for the next strike of lightning.
Hey, friends. How are things going in here? It's really nasty outside. A ghostly night. And by the way...
You should cover Rogers and throw him out to sea. They say that the dead don't sail well and that they seek revenge on their murderers.
Ro-Rogers wasn't murdered.
Yes, I was. You poisoned me.

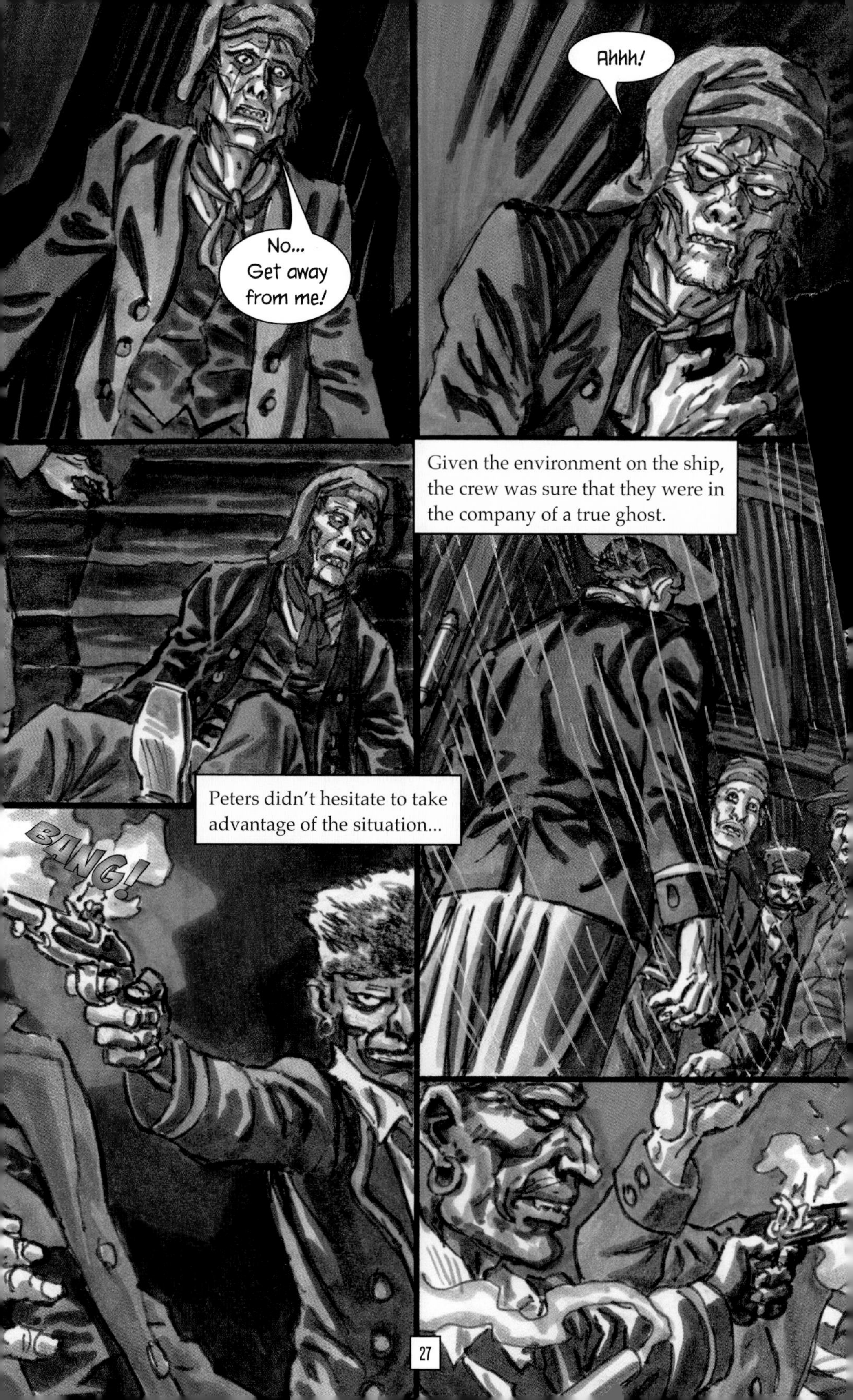
No...
Get away
from me!
Ahhh!
Given the environment on the ship, the crew was sure that they were in the company of a true ghost.
Peters didn't hesitate to take advantage of the situation...
BANG!

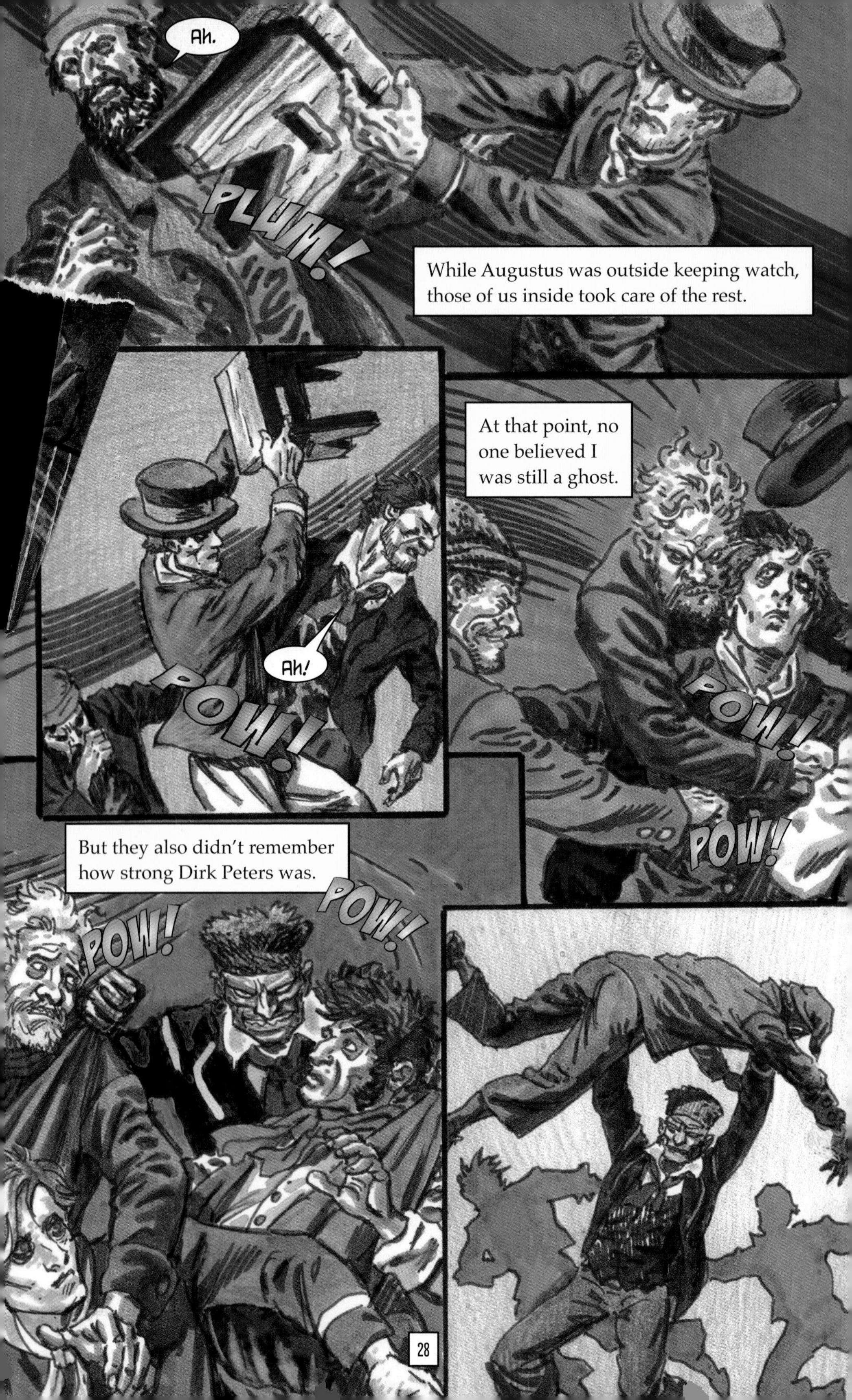

Ah.
PLUM!
While Augustus was outside keeping watch, those of us inside took care of the rest.
Ah!
POW!
At that point, no one believed I was still a ghost.
POW!
POW!
But they also didn't remember how strong Dirk Peters was.
POW!
POW!

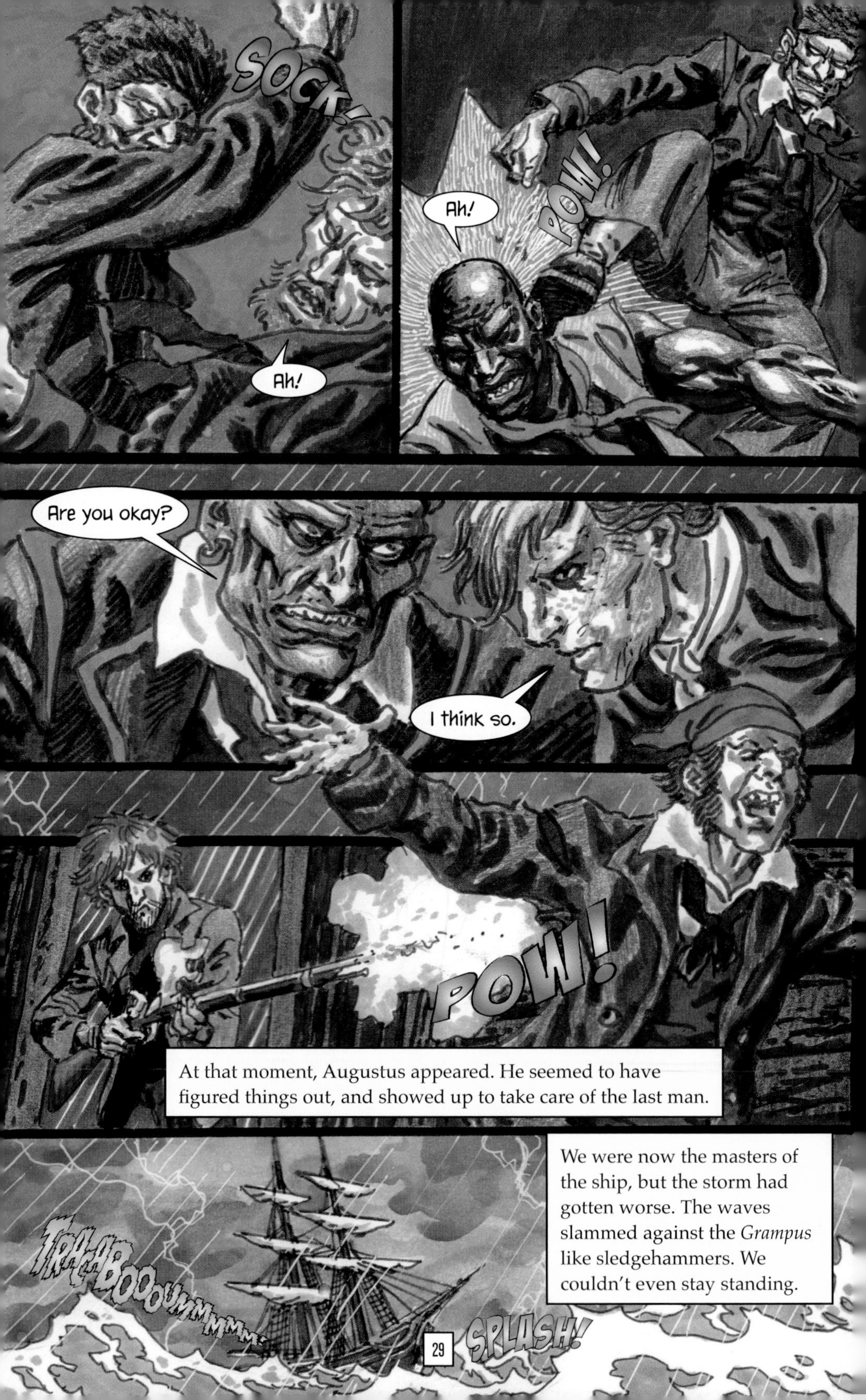
SOCK!
Ah!
Ah!
POW!
Are you okay?
I think so.
POW!
At that moment, Augustus appeared. He seemed to have figured things out, and showed up to take care of the last man.
We were now the masters of the ship, but the storm had gotten worse. The waves slammed against the *Grampus* like sledgehammers. We couldn't even stay standing.
SPLASH!

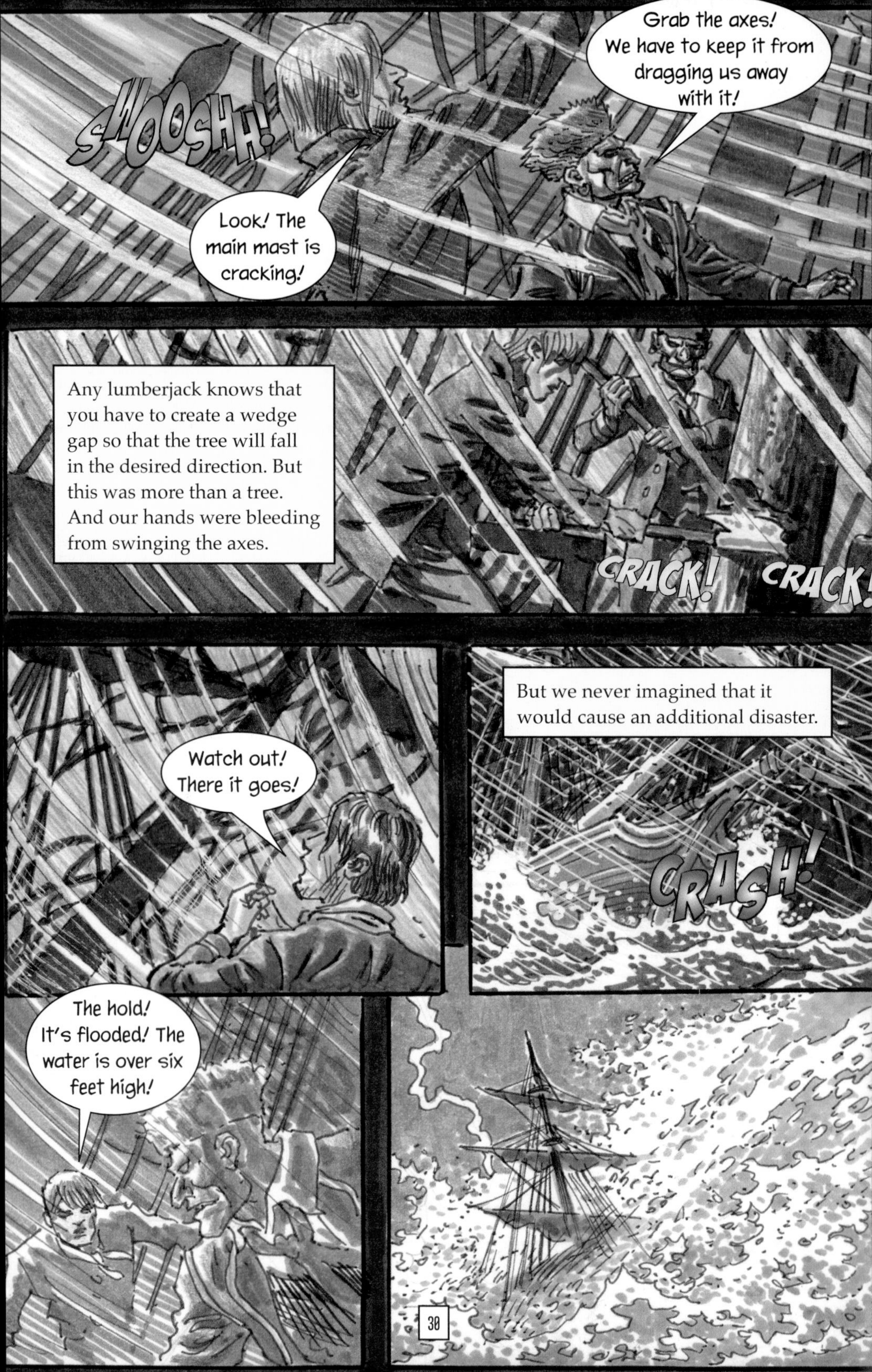
SWOOSHH!
Grab the axes! We have to keep it from dragging us away with it!
Look! The main mast is cracking!
Any lumberjack knows that you have to create a wedge gap so that the tree will fall in the desired direction. But this was more than a tree. And our hands were bleeding from swinging the axes.
CRACK!
CRACK!
Watch out! There it goes!
But we never imagined that it would cause an additional disaster.
CRASH!
The hold! It's flooded! The water is over six feet high!

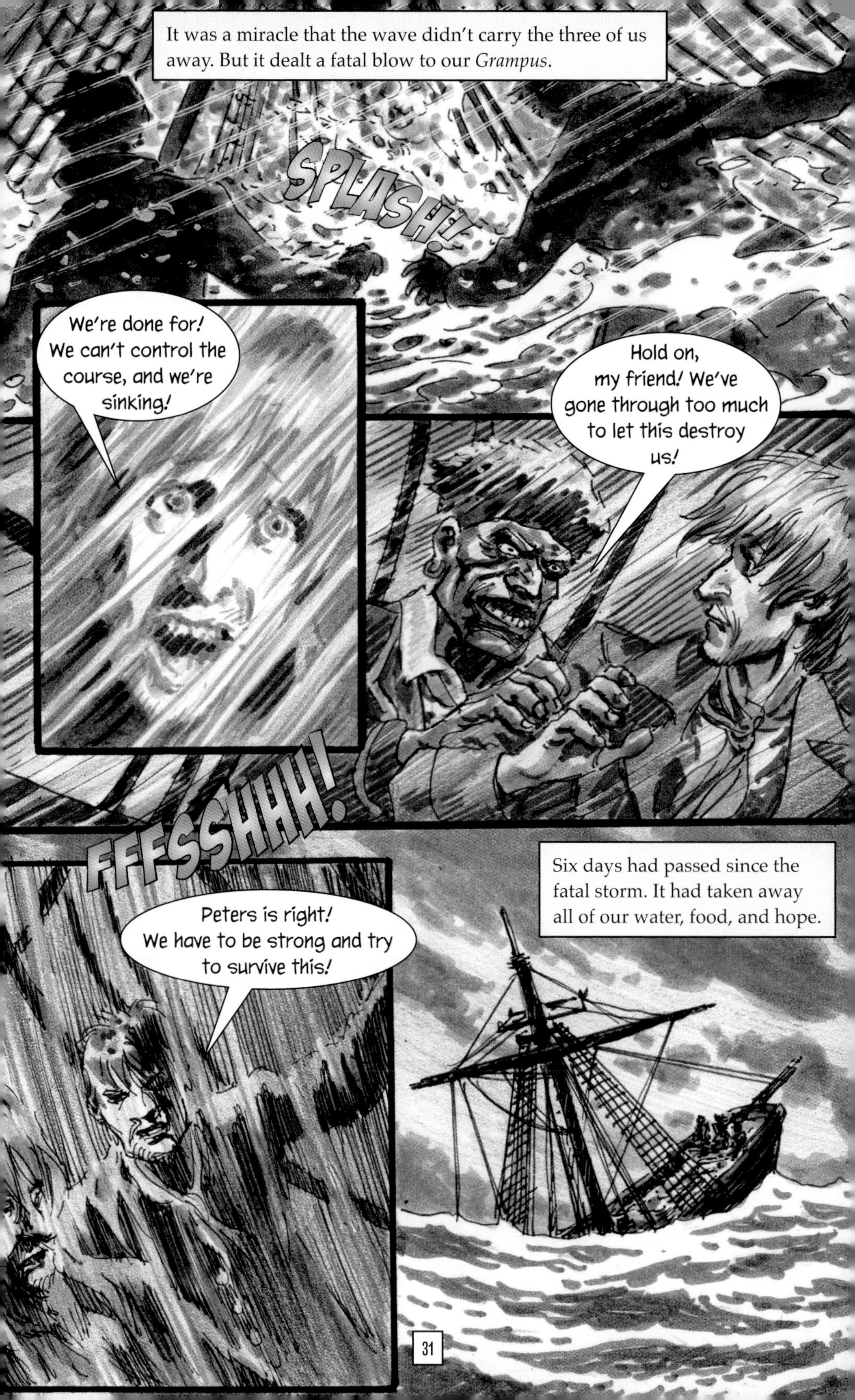
It was a miracle that the wave didn't carry the three of us away. But it dealt a fatal blow to our *Grampus*.
SPLASH!
We're done for! We can't control the course, and we're sinking!
Hold on, my friend! We've gone through too much to let this destroy us!
FFFSSHHH!
Peters is right! We have to be strong and try to survive this!
Six days had passed since the fatal storm. It had taken away all of our water, food, and hope.

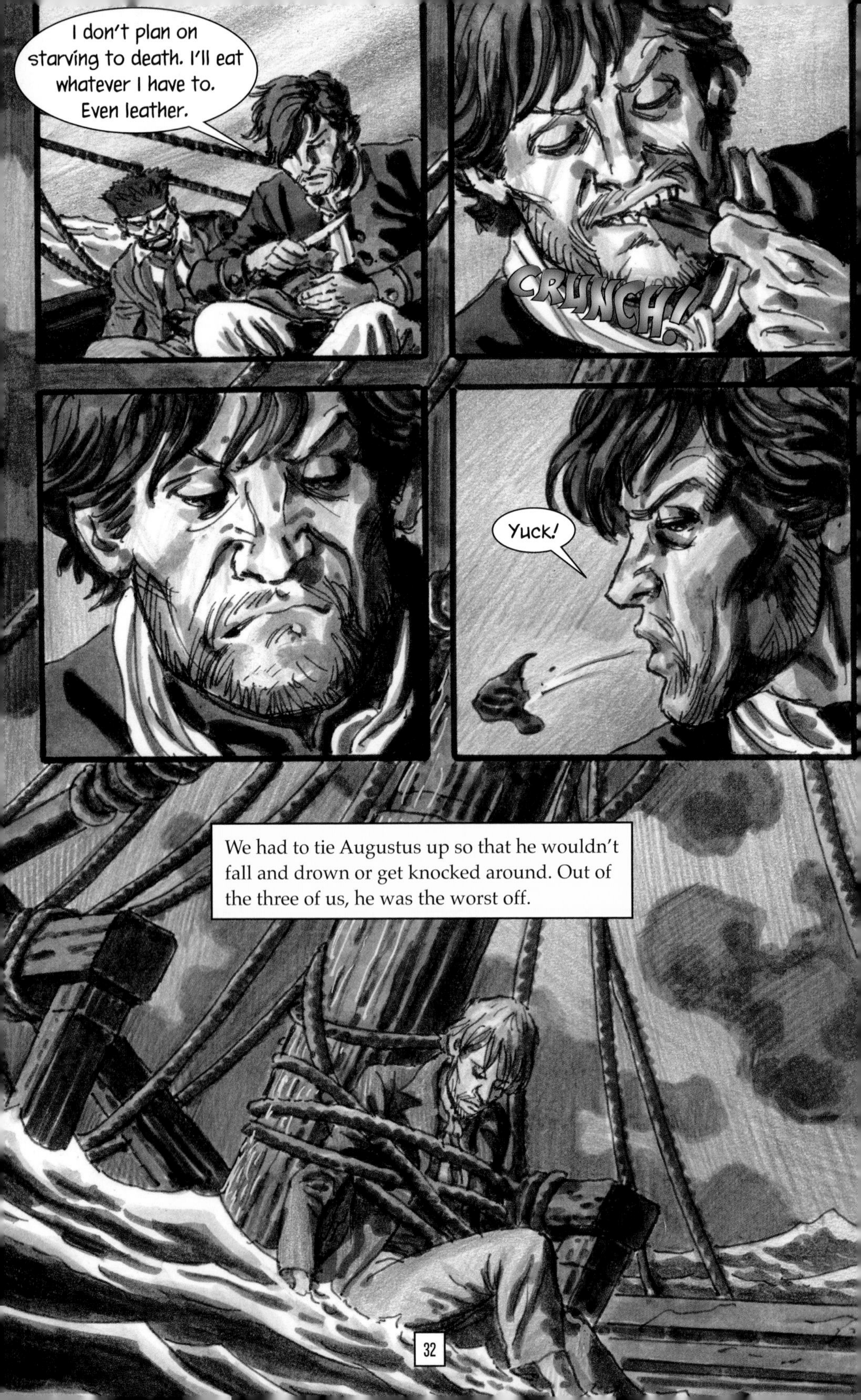
I don't plan on starving to death. I'll eat whatever I have to. Even leather.
CRUNCH!!
Yuck!
We had to tie Augustus up so that he wouldn't fall and drown or get knocked around. Out of the three of us, he was the worst off.

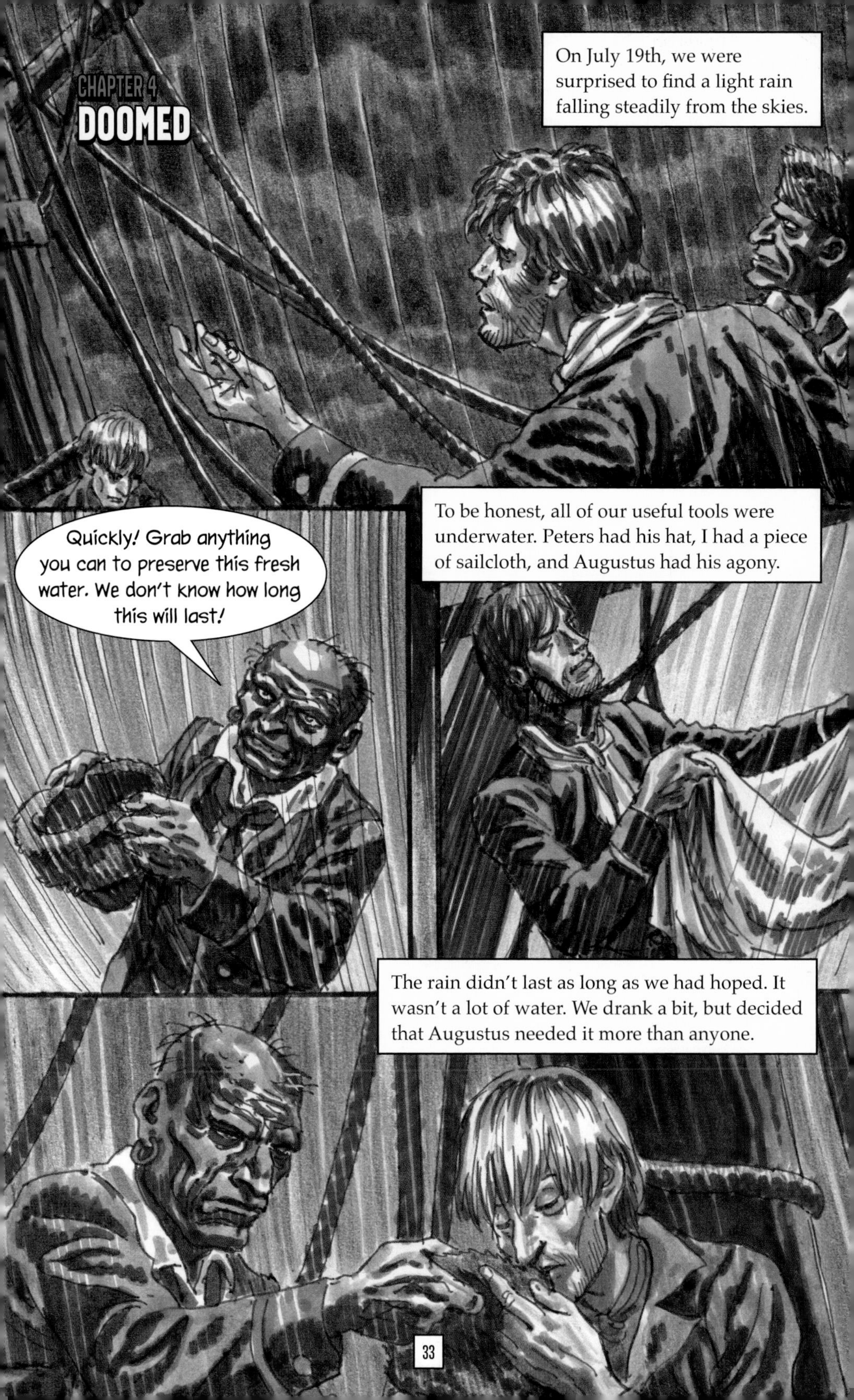
CHAPTER 4
DOOMED
On July 19th, we were surprised to find a light rain falling steadily from the skies.
To be honest, all of our useful tools were underwater. Peters had his hat, I had a piece of sailcloth, and Augustus had his agony.
Quickly! Grab anything you can to preserve this fresh water. We don't know how long this will last!
The rain didn't last as long as we had hoped. It wasn't a lot of water. We drank a bit, but decided that Augustus needed it more than anyone.

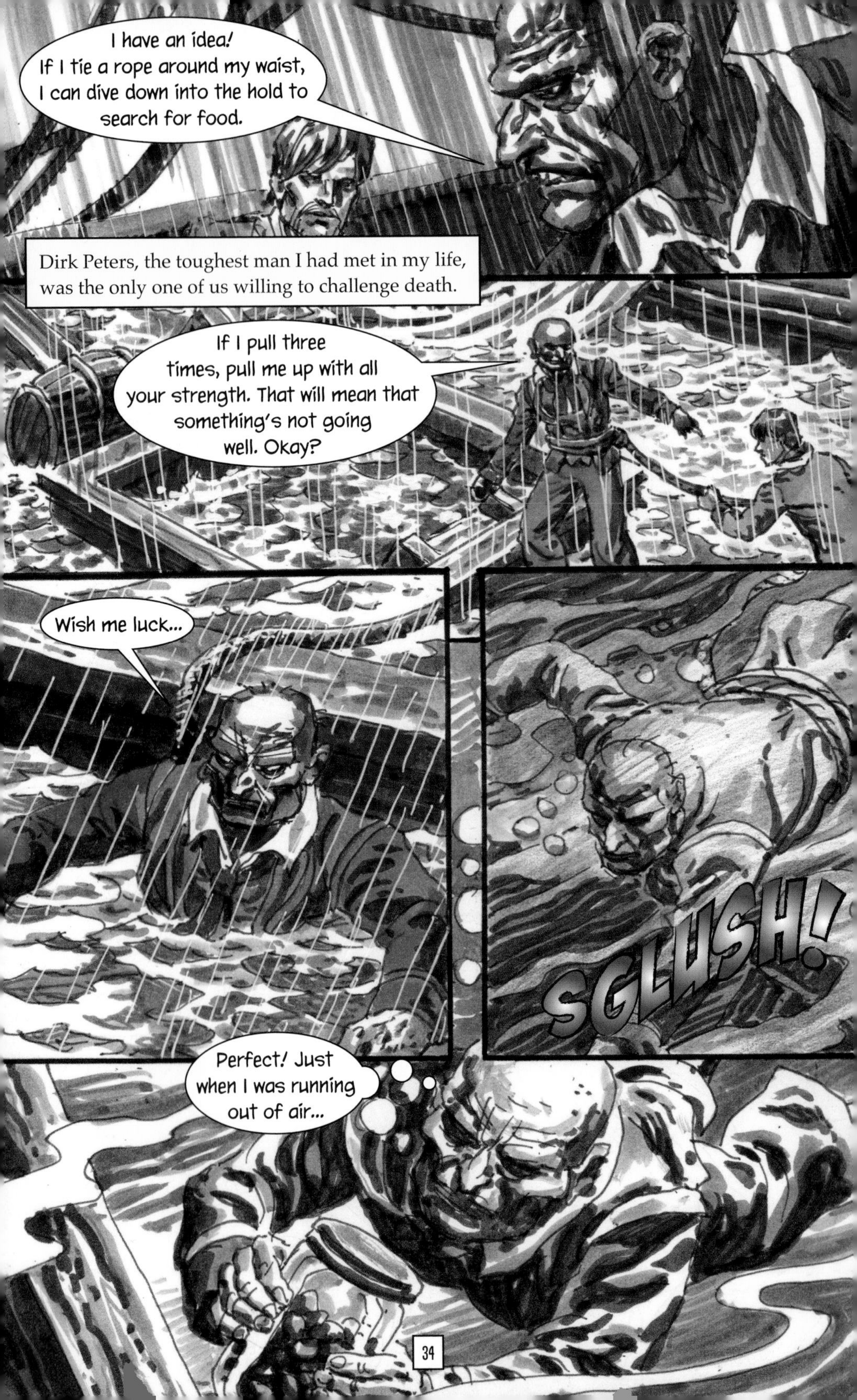
I have an idea! If I tie a rope around my waist, I can dive down into the hold to search for food.
Dirk Peters, the toughest man I had met in my life, was the only one of us willing to challenge death.
If I pull three times, pull me up with all your strength. That will mean that something's not going well. Okay?
Wish me luck...
SGLUSH!
Perfect! Just when I was running out of air...

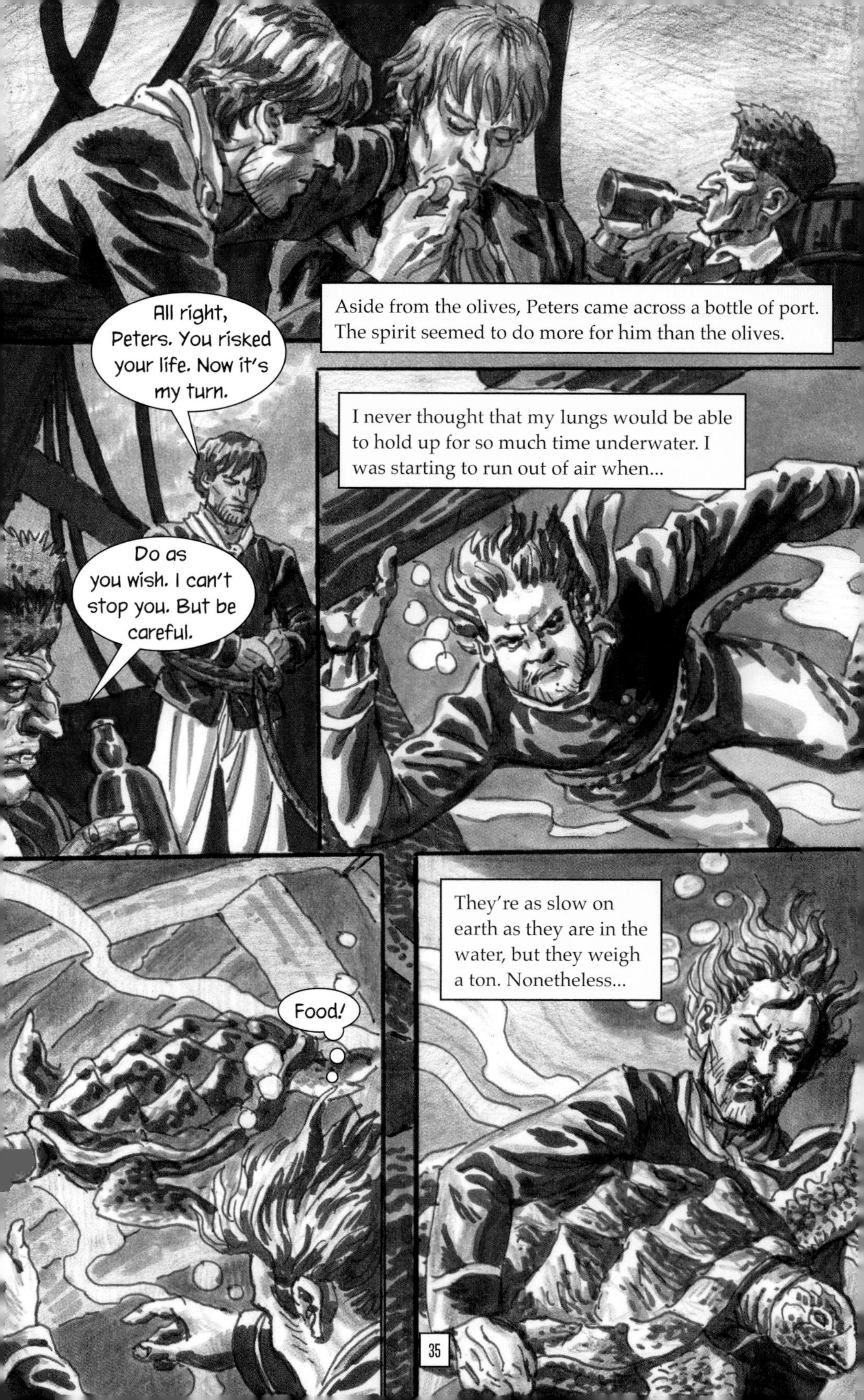
Aside from the olives, Peters came across a bottle of port. The spirit seemed to do more for him than the olives.
All right, Peters. You risked your life. Now it's my turn.
Do as you wish. I can't stop you. But be careful.
I never thought that my lungs would be able to hold up for so much time underwater. I was starting to run out of air when...
Food!
They're as slow on earth as they are in the water, but they weigh a ton. Nonetheless...

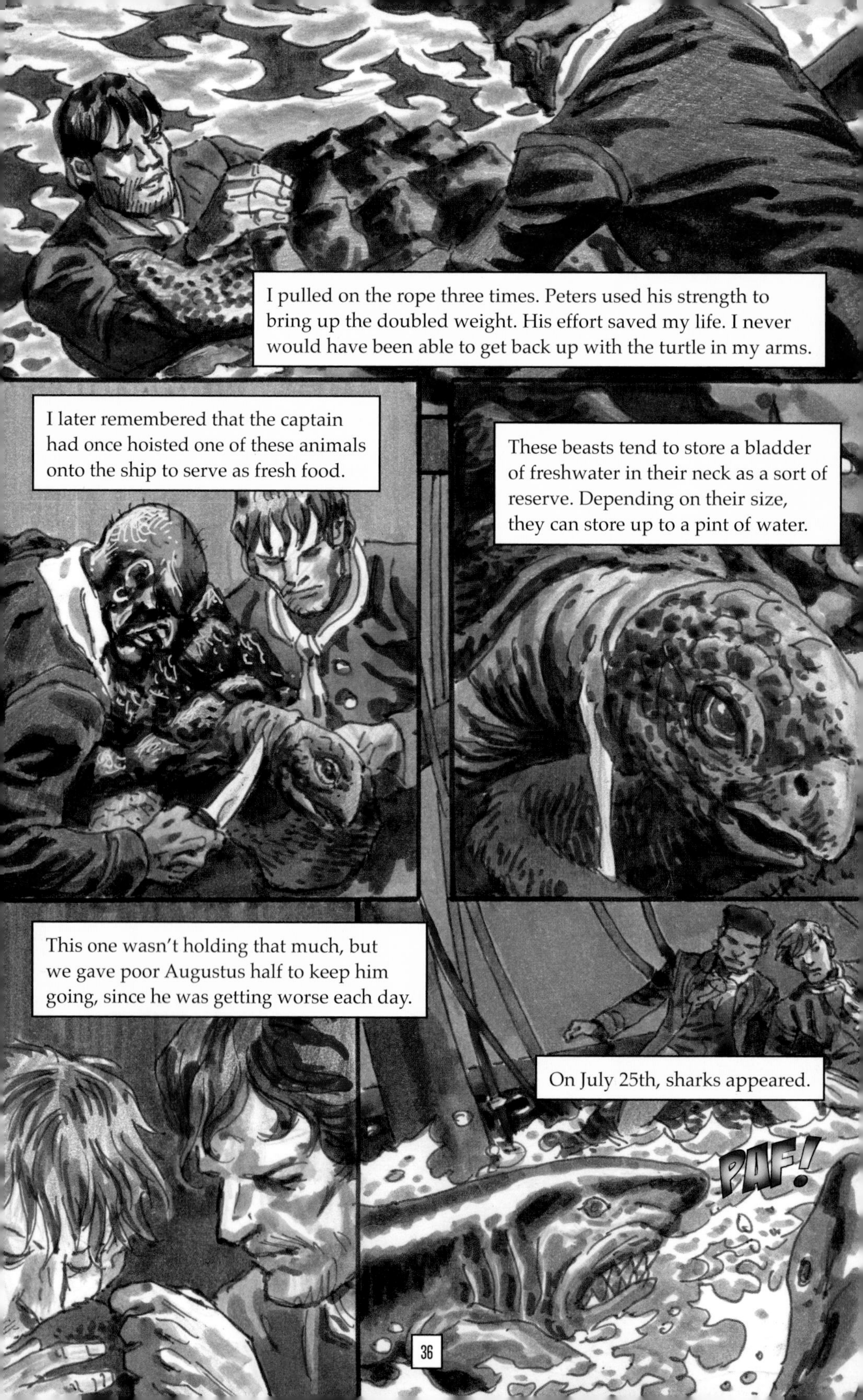
I pulled on the rope three times. Peters used his strength to bring up the doubled weight. His effort saved my life. I never would have been able to get back up with the turtle in my arms.
I later remembered that the captain had once hoisted one of these animals onto the ship to serve as fresh food.
These beasts tend to store a bladder of freshwater in their neck as a sort of reserve. Depending on their size, they can store up to a pint of water.
This one wasn't holding that much, but we gave poor Augustus half to keep him going, since he was getting worse each day.
On July 25th, sharks appeared.
PAF!

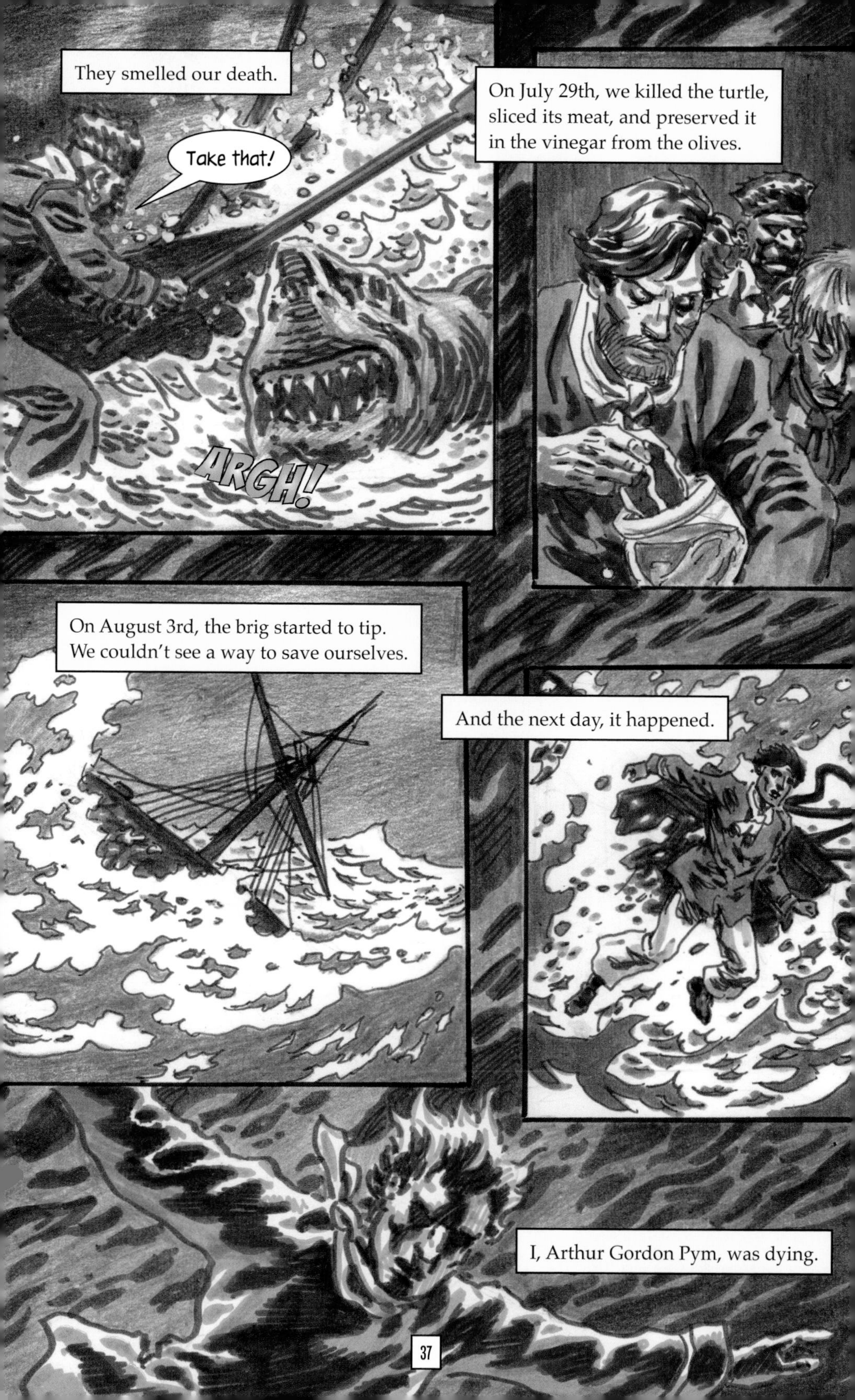
They smelled our death.
Take that!
ARGH!
On July 29th, we killed the turtle, sliced its meat, and preserved it in the vinegar from the olives.
On August 3rd, the brig started to tip. We couldn't see a way to save ourselves.
And the next day, it happened.
I, Arthur Gordon Pym, was dying.

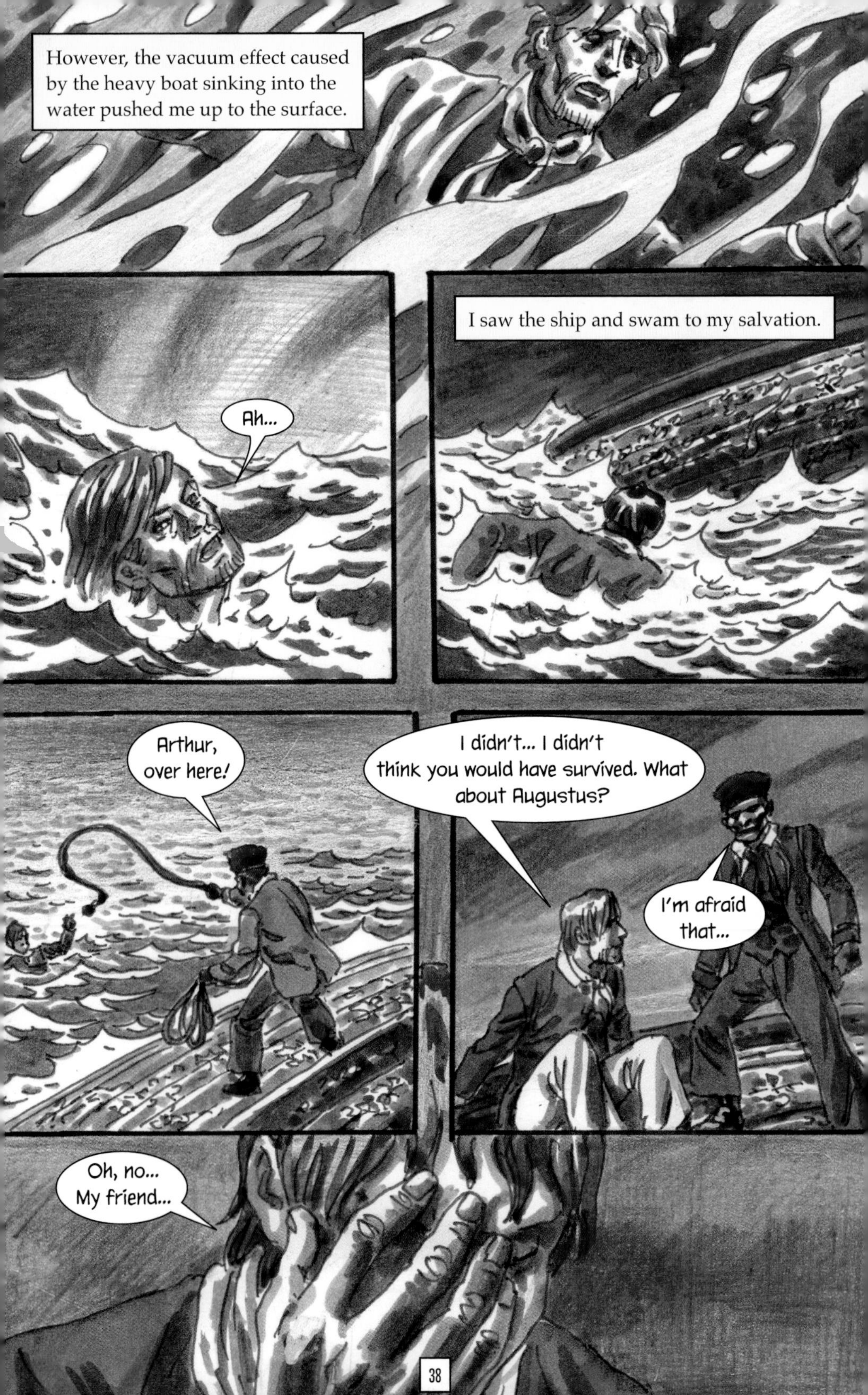
However, the vacuum effect caused by the heavy boat sinking into the water pushed me up to the surface.
Ah...
I saw the ship and swam to my salvation.
Arthur, over here!
I didn't... I didn't think you would have survived. What about Augustus?
I'm afraid that...
Oh, no... My friend...

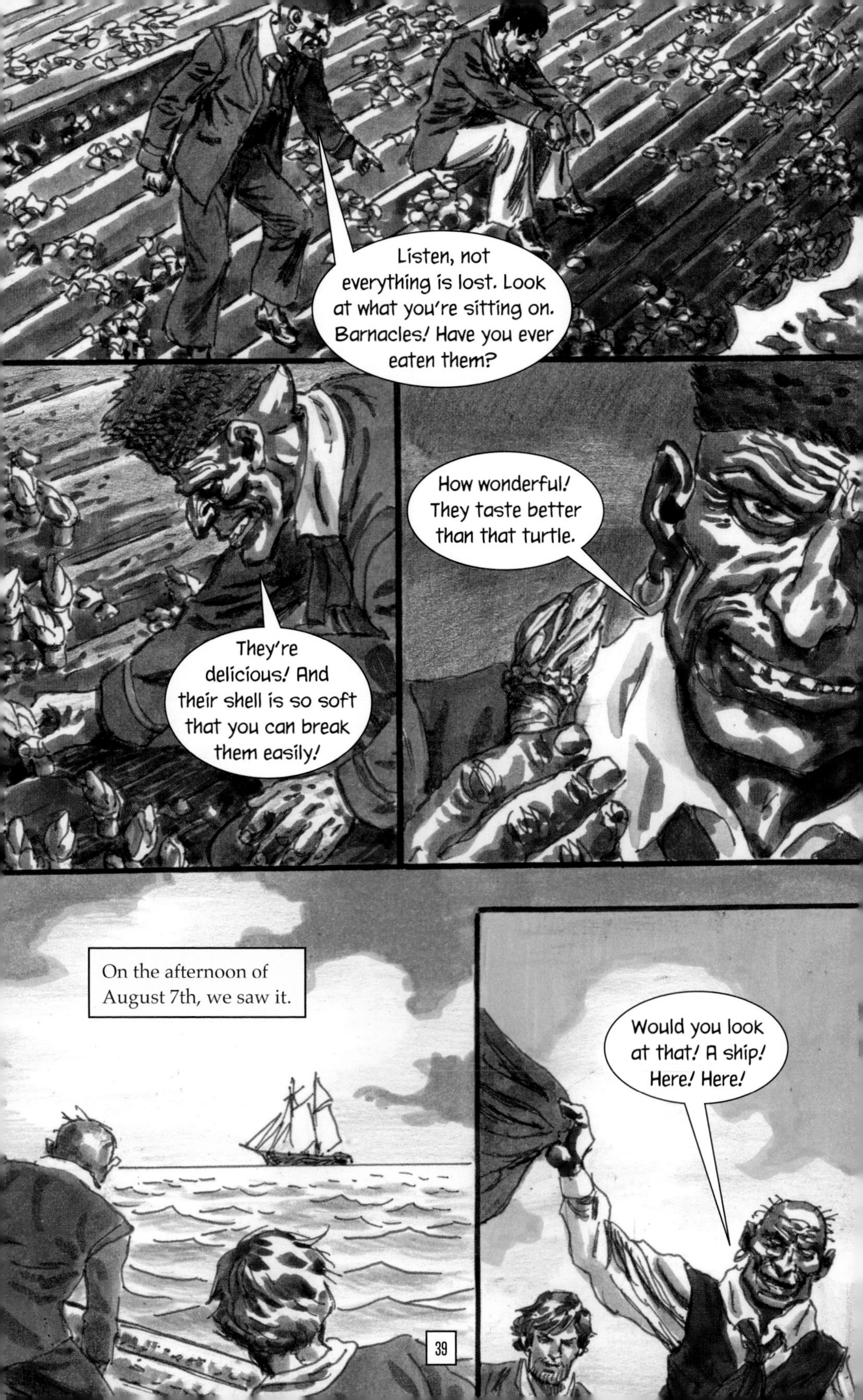
Listen, not everything is lost. Look at what you're sitting on. Barnacles! Have you ever eaten them?
They're delicious! And their shell is so soft that you can break them easily!
How wonderful! They taste better than that turtle.
On the afternoon of August 7th, we saw it.
Would you look at that! A ship! Here! Here!

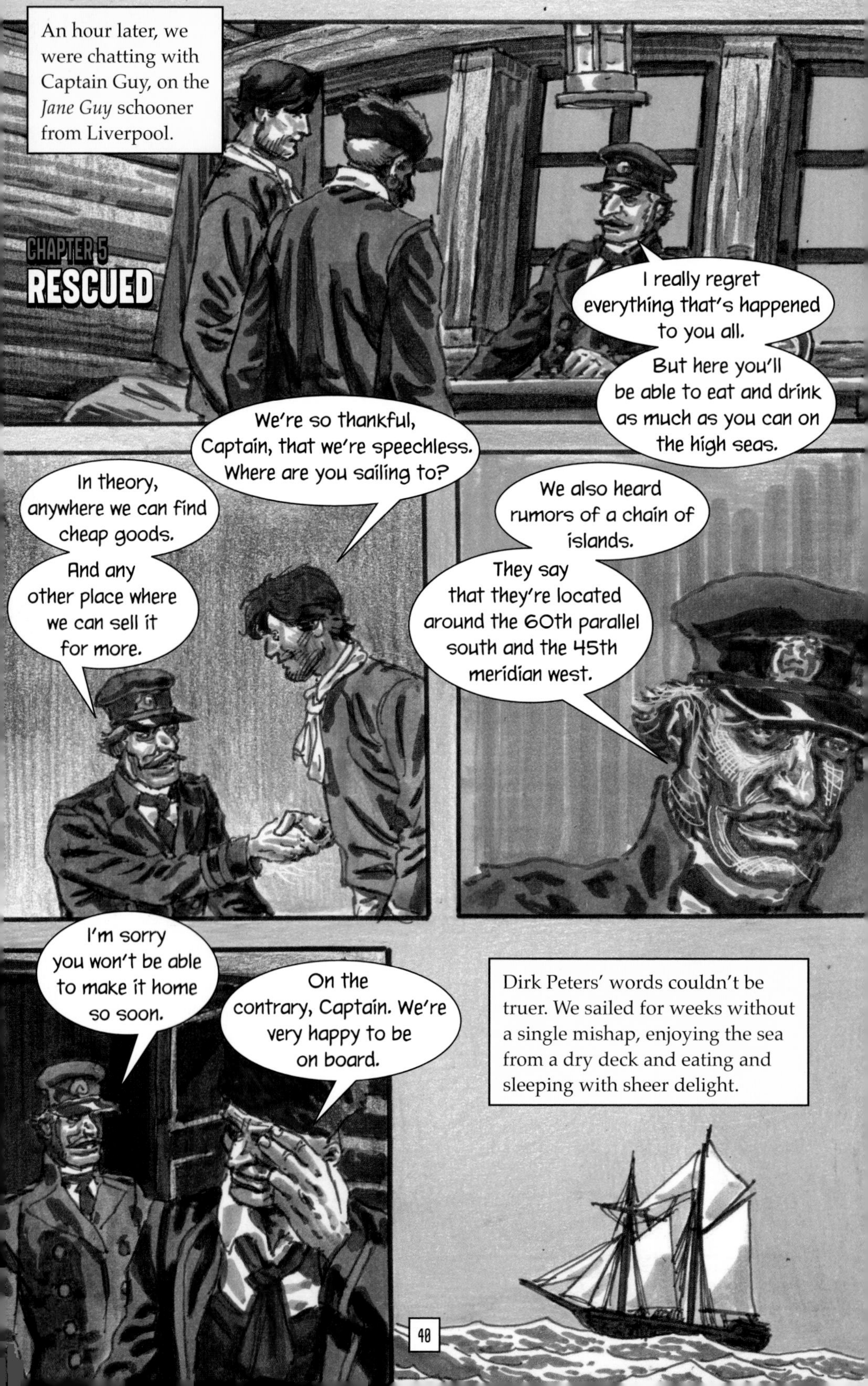
An hour later, we were chatting with Captain Guy, on the *Jane Guy* schooner from Liverpool.
CHAPTER 5
RESCUED
I really regret everything that's happened to you all.
But here you'll be able to eat and drink as much as you can on the high seas.
We're so thankful, Captain, that we're speechless. Where are you sailing to?
In theory, anywhere we can find cheap goods.
And any other place where we can sell it for more.
We also heard rumors of a chain of islands.
They say that they're located around the 60th parallel south and the 45th meridian west.
I'm sorry you won't be able to make it home so soon.
On the contrary, Captain. We're very happy to be on board.
Dirk Peters' words couldn't be truer. We sailed for weeks without a single mishap, enjoying the sea from a dry deck and eating and sleeping with sheer delight.

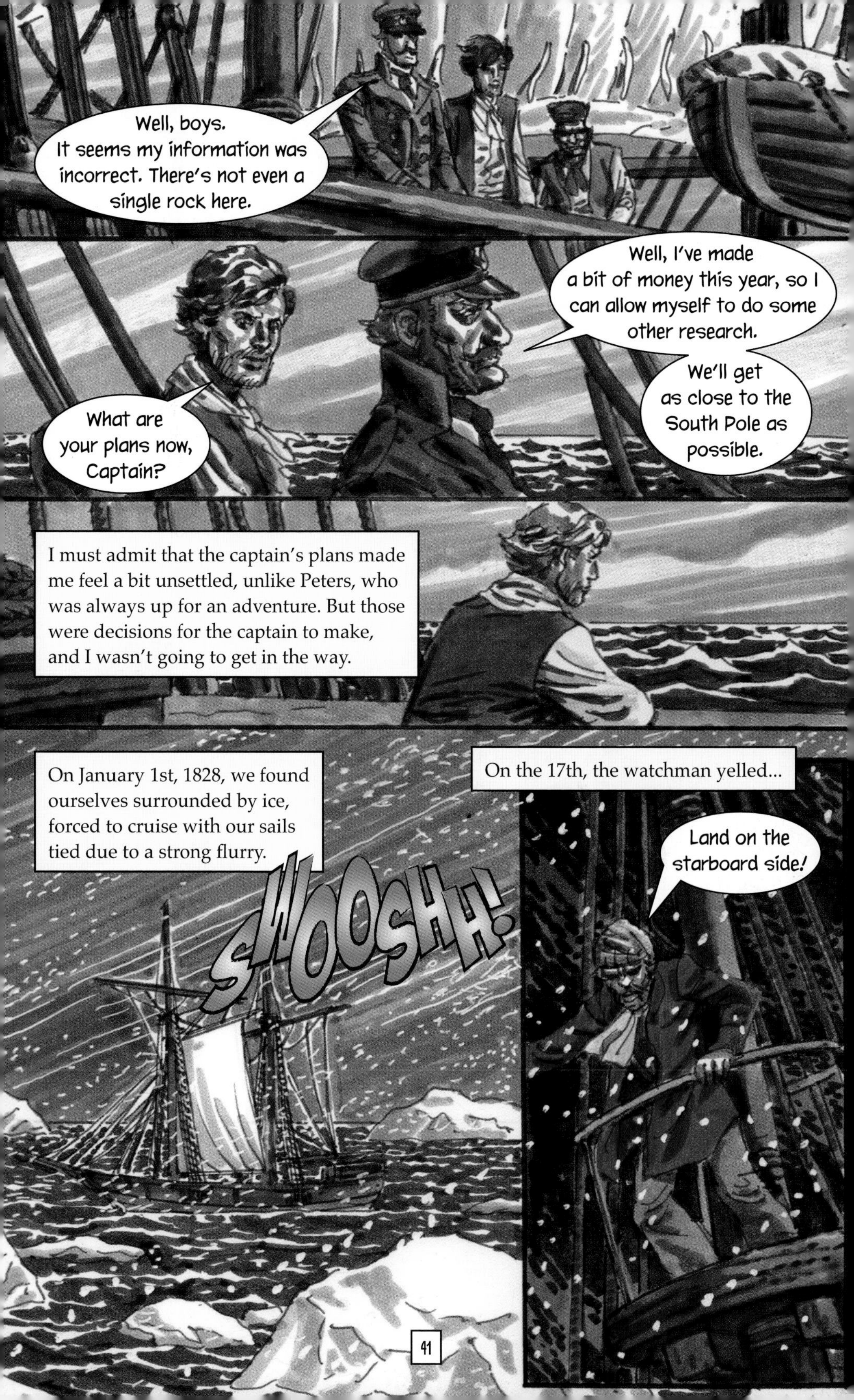
Well, boys. It seems my information was incorrect. There's not even a single rock here.
What are your plans now, Captain?
Well, I've made a bit of money this year, so I can allow myself to do some other research.
We'll get as close to the South Pole as possible.
I must admit that the captain's plans made me feel a bit unsettled, unlike Peters, who was always up for an adventure. But those were decisions for the captain to make, and I wasn't going to get in the way.
On January 1st, 1828, we found ourselves surrounded by ice, forced to cruise with our sails tied due to a strong flurry.
SWOOSHH!
On the 17th, the watchman yelled...
Land on the starboard side!

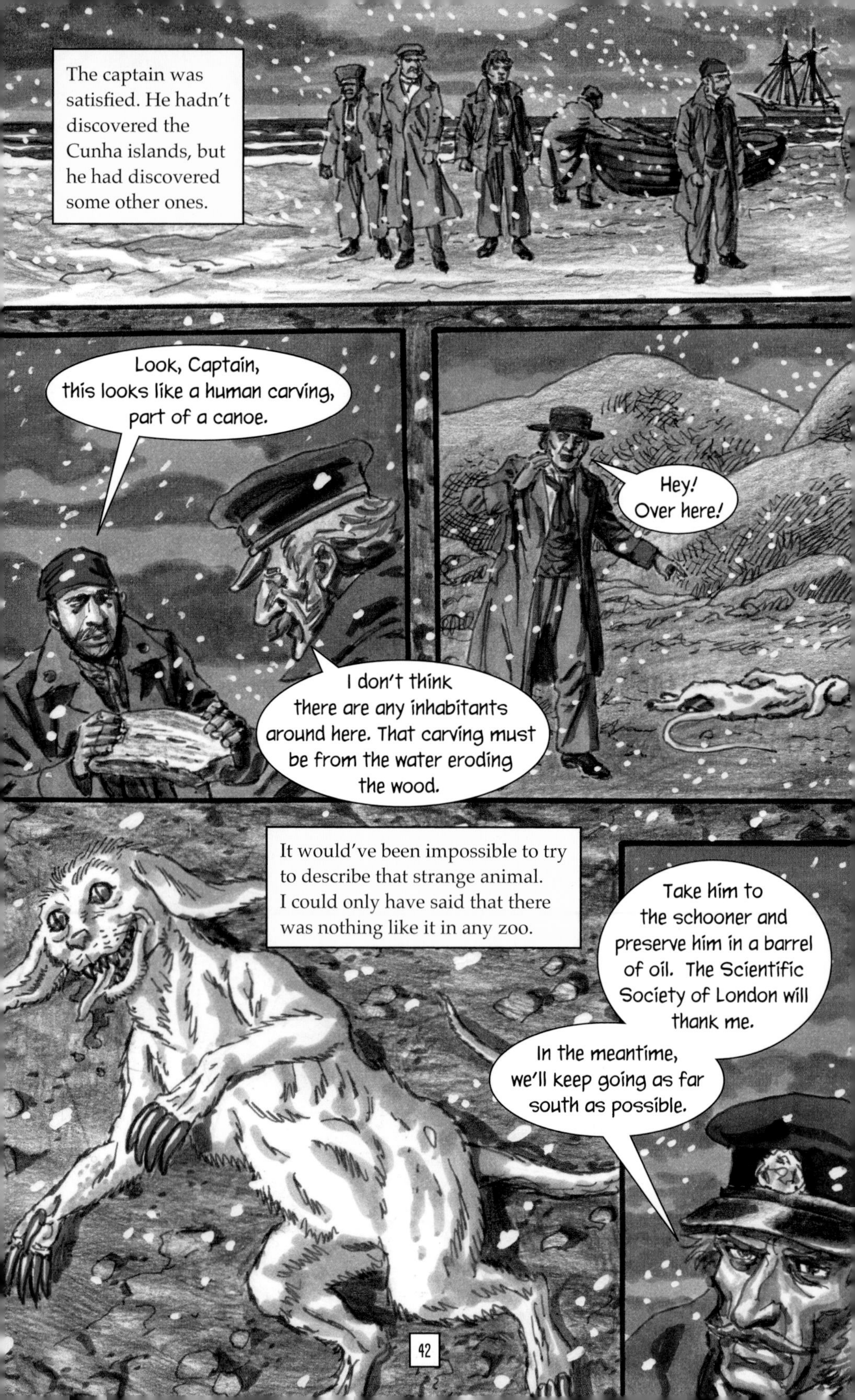
The captain was satisfied. He hadn't discovered the Cunha islands, but he had discovered some other ones.
Look, Captain, this looks like a human carving, part of a canoe.
I don't think there are any inhabitants around here. That carving must be from the water eroding the wood.
Hey! Over here!
It would've been impossible to try to describe that strange animal. I could only have said that there was nothing like it in any zoo.
Take him to the schooner and preserve him in a barrel of oil. The Scientific Society of London will thank me.
In the meantime, we'll keep going as far south as possible.

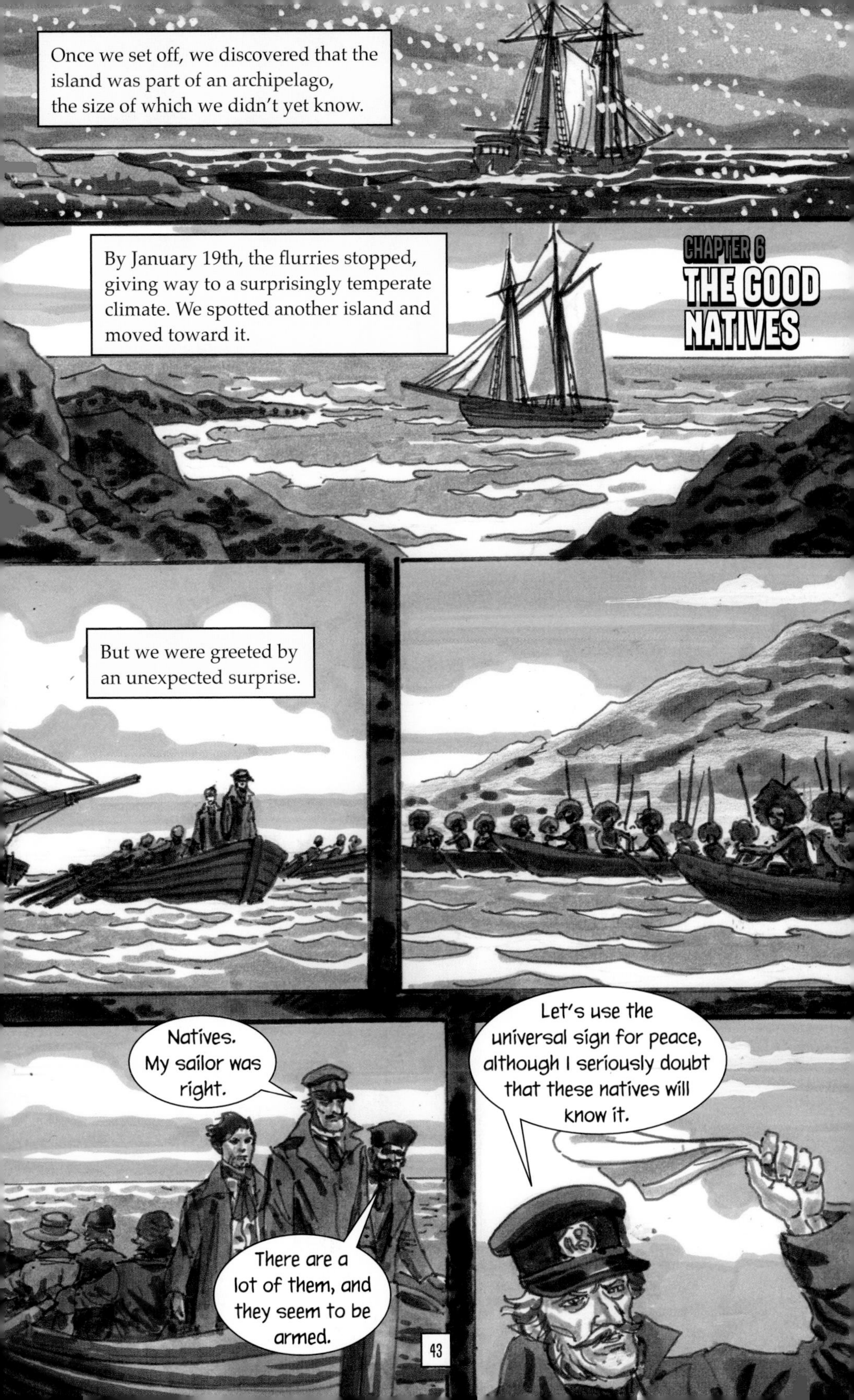
Once we set off, we discovered that the island was part of an archipelago, the size of which we didn't yet know.
By January 19th, the flurries stopped, giving way to a surprisingly temperate climate. We spotted another island and moved toward it.
CHAPTER 6
THE GOOD NATIVES
But we were greeted by an unexpected surprise.
Natives. My sailor was right.
There are a lot of them, and they seem to be armed.
Let's use the universal sign for peace, although I seriously doubt that these natives will know it.

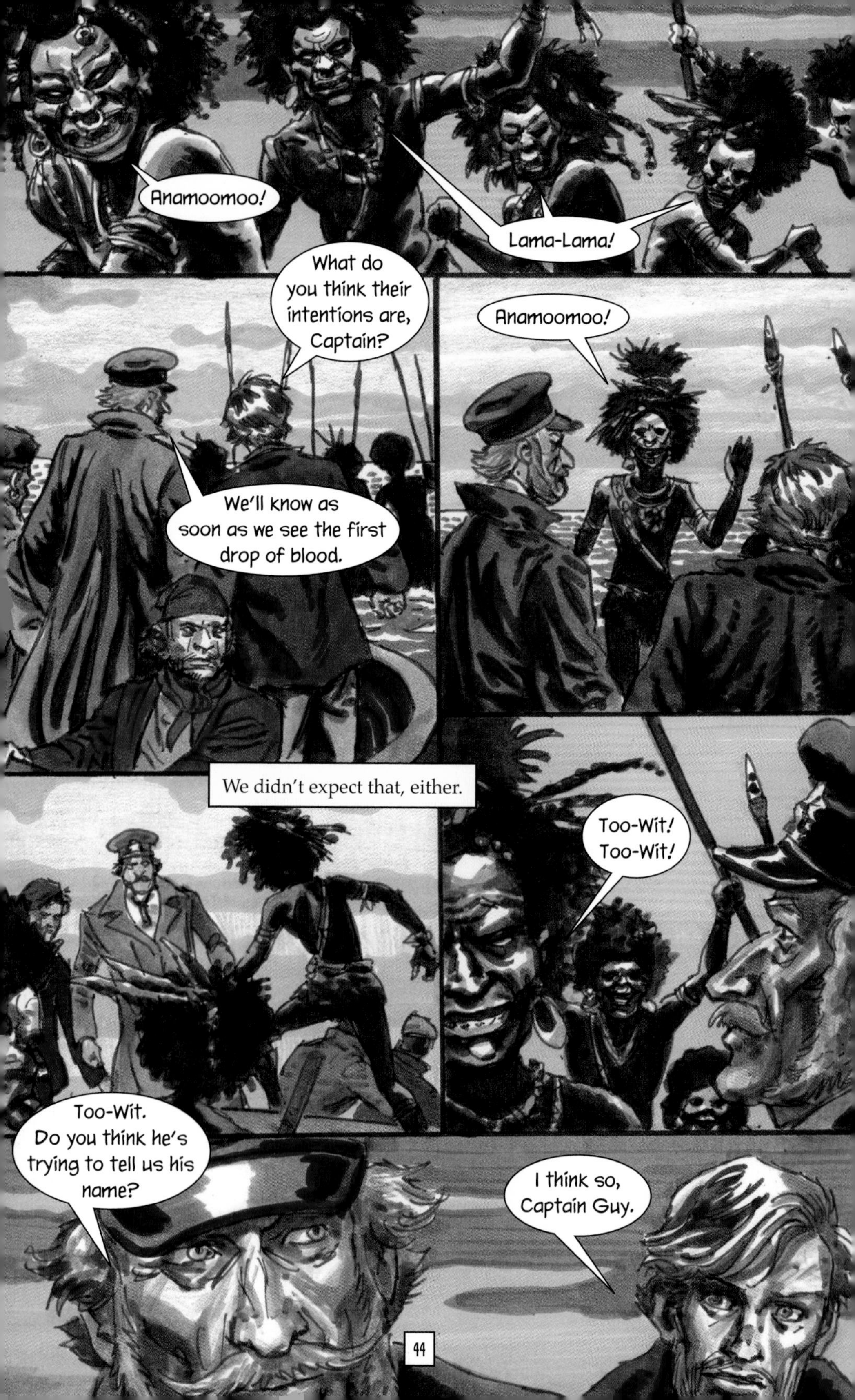
Anamoomoo!
Lama-Lama!
What do you think their intentions are, Captain?
We'll know as soon as we see the first drop of blood.
Anamoomoo!
We didn't expect that, either.
Too-Wit! Too-Wit!
Too-Wit. Do you think he's trying to tell us his name?
I think so, Captain Guy.

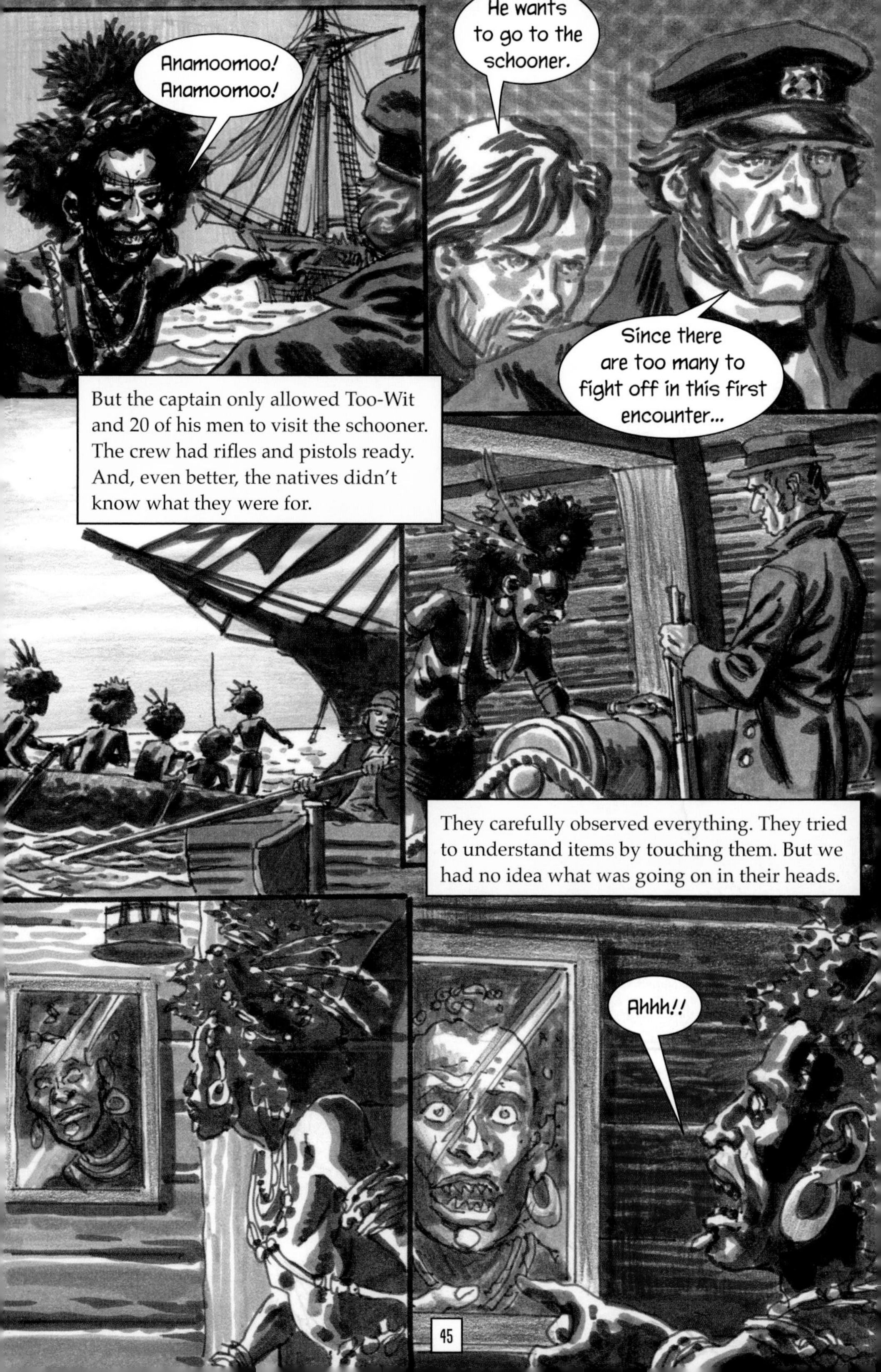
Anamoomoo! Anamoomoo!
He wants to go to the schooner.
Since there are too many to fight off in this first encounter...
But the captain only allowed Too-Wit and 20 of his men to visit the schooner. The crew had rifles and pistols ready. And, even better, the natives didn't know what they were for.
They carefully observed everything. They tried to understand items by touching them. But we had no idea what was going on in their heads.
Ahhh!!

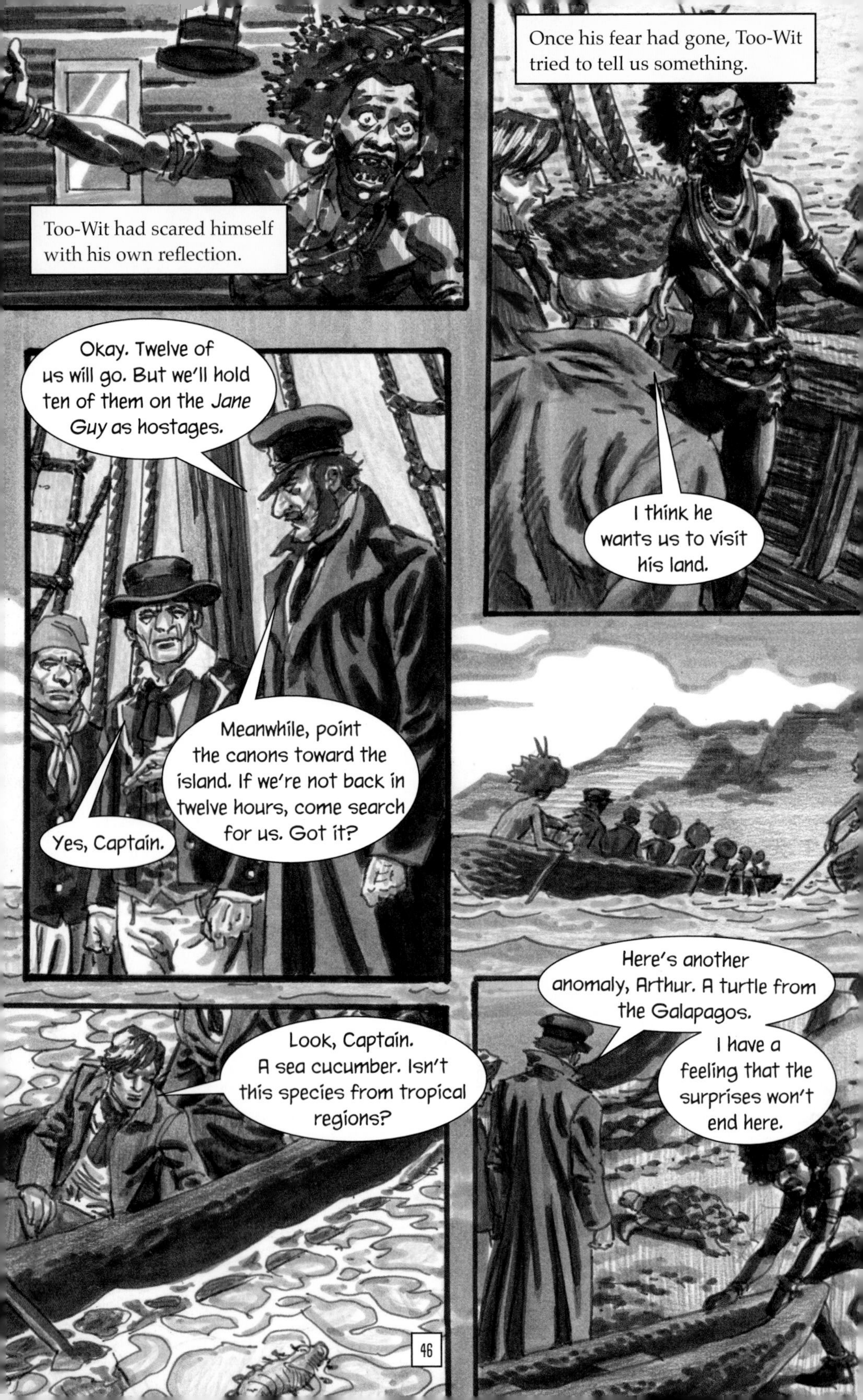
Too-Wit had scared himself with his own reflection.
Once his fear had gone, Too-Wit tried to tell us something.
I think he wants us to visit his land.
Okay. Twelve of us will go. But we'll hold ten of them on the *Jane Guy* as hostages.
Meanwhile, point the canons toward the island. If we're not back in twelve hours, come search for us. Got it?
Yes, Captain.
Look, Captain. A sea cucumber. Isn't this species from tropical regions?
Here's another anomaly, Arthur. A turtle from the Galapagos.
I have a feeling that the surprises won't end here.
46

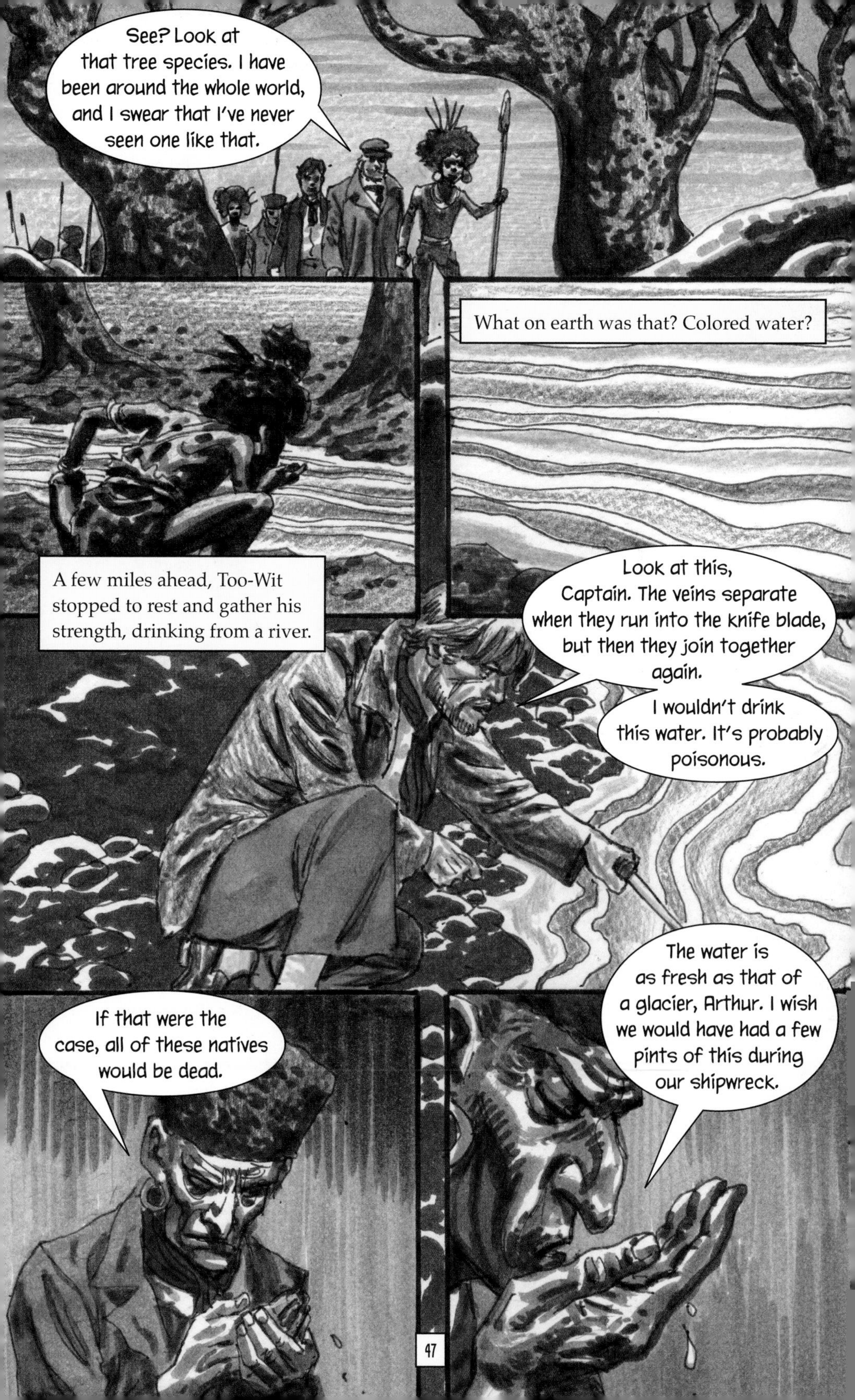

See? Look at that tree species. I have been around the whole world, and I swear that I've never seen one like that.
What on earth was that? Colored water?
A few miles ahead, Too-Wit stopped to rest and gather his strength, drinking from a river.
Look at this, Captain. The veins separate when they run into the knife blade, but then they join together again.
I wouldn't drink this water. It's probably poisonous.
If that were the case, all of these natives would be dead.
The water is as fresh as that of a glacier, Arthur. I wish we would have had a few pints of this during our shipwreck.

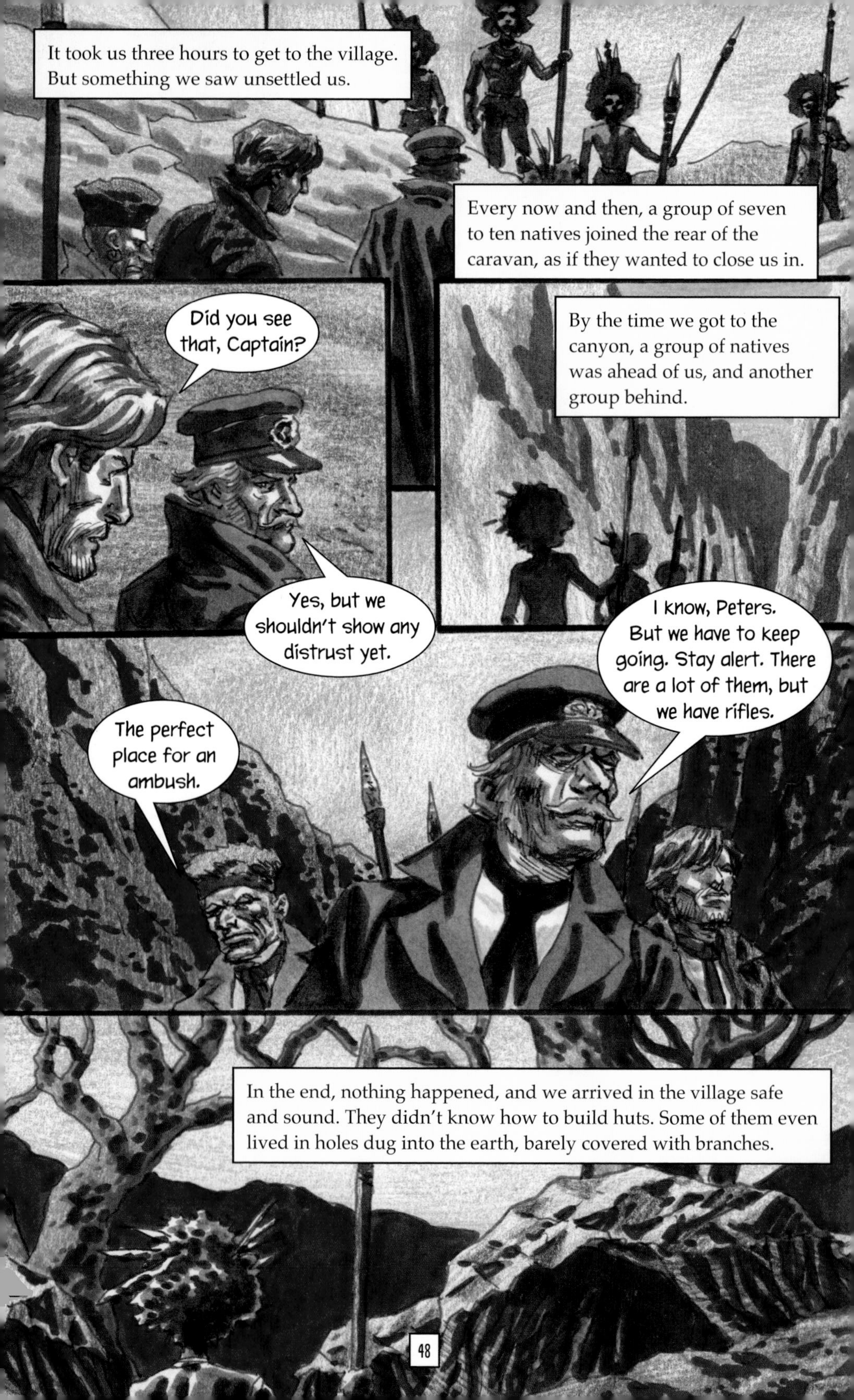
It took us three hours to get to the village. But something we saw unsettled us.
Every now and then, a group of seven to ten natives joined the rear of the caravan, as if they wanted to close us in.
Did you see that, Captain?
Yes, but we shouldn't show any distrust yet.
By the time we got to the canyon, a group of natives was ahead of us, and another group behind.
The perfect place for an ambush.
I know, Peters. But we have to keep going. Stay alert. There are a lot of them, but we have rifles.
In the end, nothing happened, and we arrived in the village safe and sound. They didn't know how to build huts. Some of them even lived in holes dug into the earth, barely covered with branches.

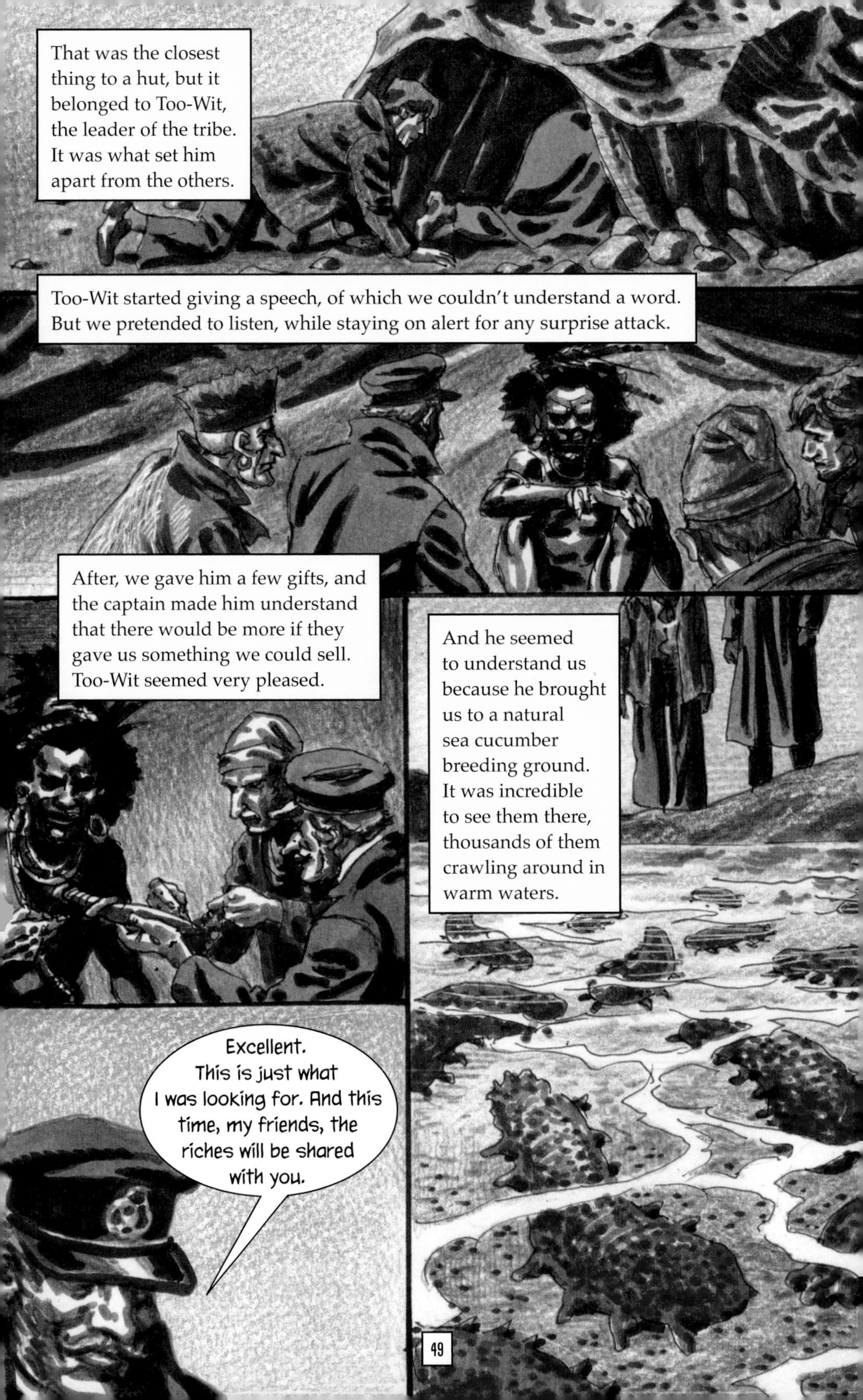
That was the closest thing to a hut, but it belonged to Too-Wit, the leader of the tribe. It was what set him apart from the others.
Too-Wit started giving a speech, of which we couldn't understand a word. But we pretended to listen, while staying on alert for any surprise attack.
After, we gave him a few gifts, and the captain made him understand that there would be more if they gave us something we could sell. Too-Wit seemed very pleased.
And he seemed to understand us because he brought us to a natural sea cucumber breeding ground. It was incredible to see them there, thousands of them crawling around in warm waters.
Excellent. This is just what I was looking for. And this time, my friends, the riches will be shared with you.

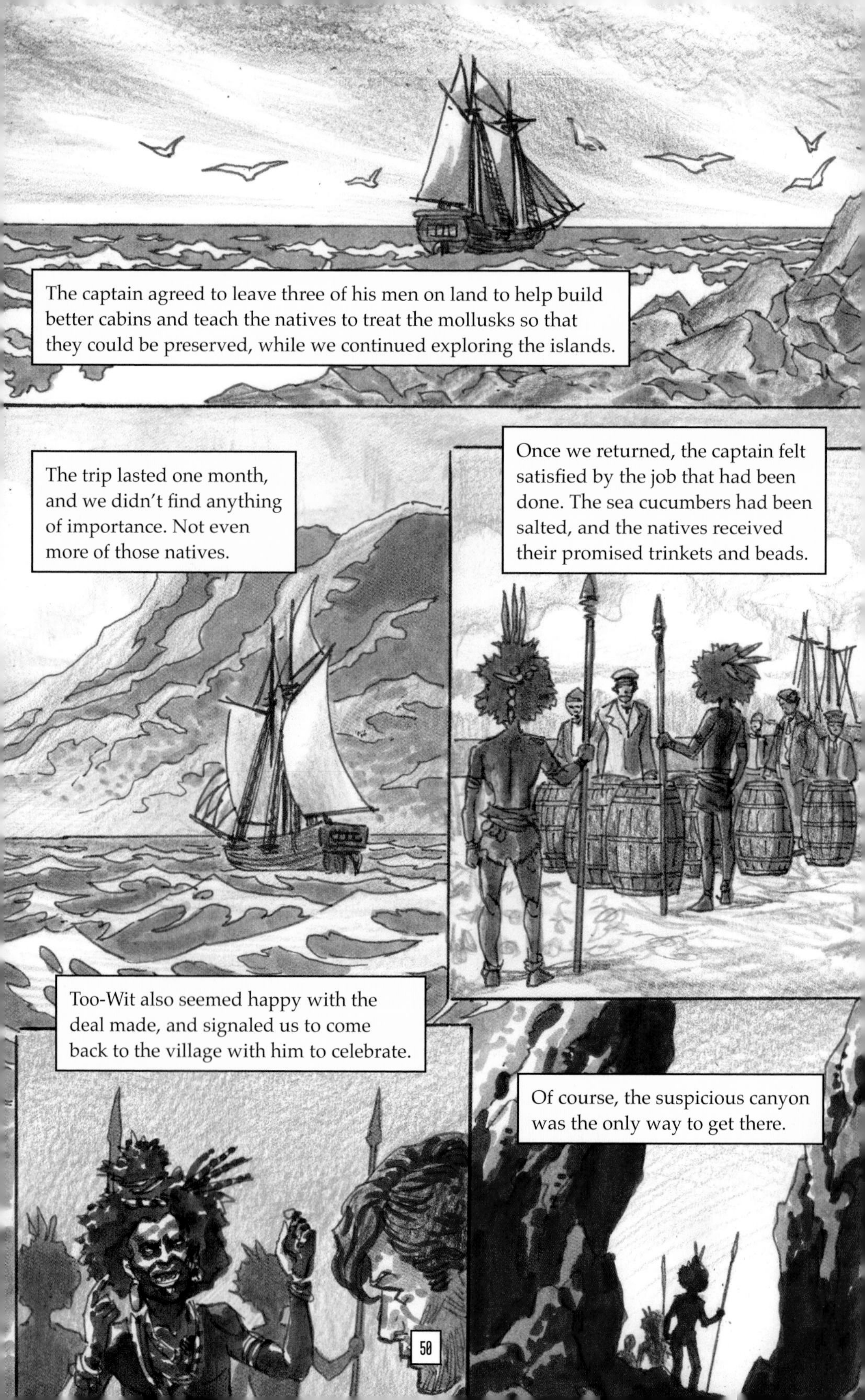
The captain agreed to leave three of his men on land to help build better cabins and teach the natives to treat the mollusks so that they could be preserved, while we continued exploring the islands.
The trip lasted one month, and we didn't find anything of importance. Not even more of those natives.
Once we returned, the captain felt satisfied by the job that had been done. The sea cucumbers had been salted, and the natives received their promised trinkets and beads.
Too-Wit also seemed happy with the deal made, and signaled us to come back to the village with him to celebrate.
Of course, the suspicious canyon was the only way to get there.

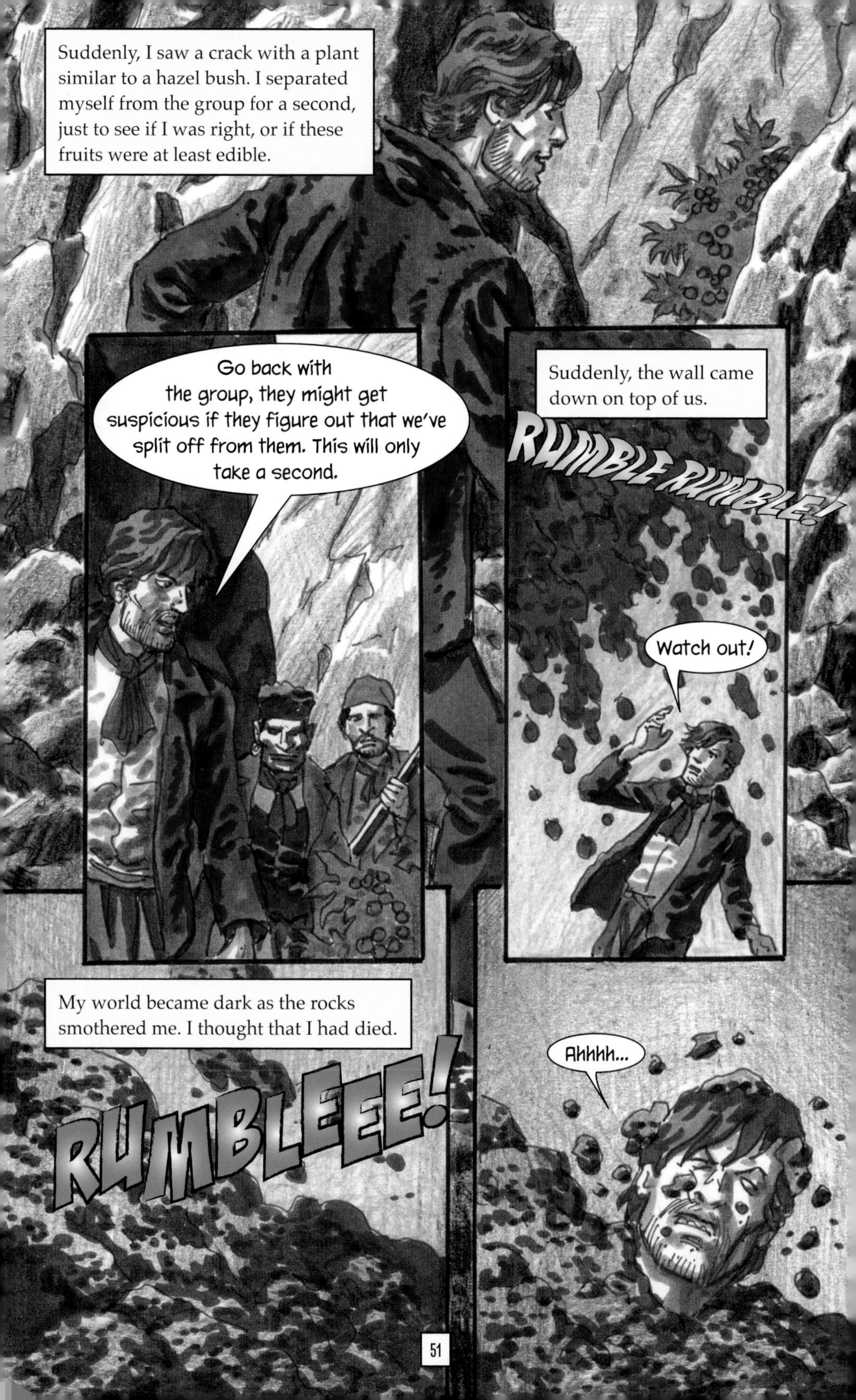
Suddenly, I saw a crack with a plant similar to a hazel bush. I separated myself from the group for a second, just to see if I was right, or if these fruits were at least edible.
Go back with the group, they might get suspicious if they figure out that we've split off from them. This will only take a second.
Suddenly, the wall came down on top of us.
RUMBLE RUMBLE!
Watch out!
My world became dark as the rocks smothered me. I thought that I had died.
RUMBLEEE!
Ahhhh...

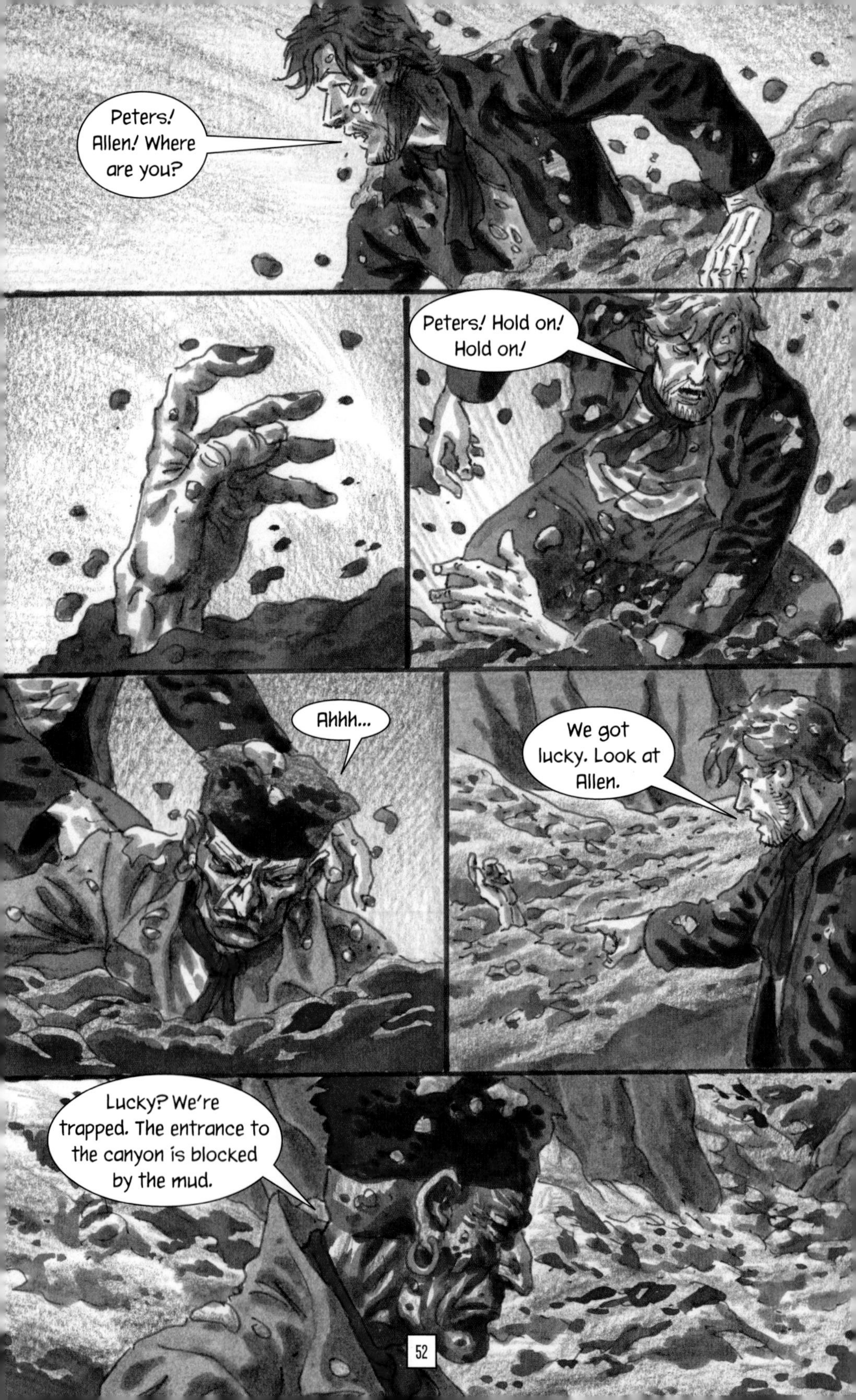
Peters! Allen! Where are you?
Peters! Hold on! Hold on!
Ahhh...
We got lucky. Look at Allen.
Lucky? We're trapped. The entrance to the canyon is blocked by the mud.

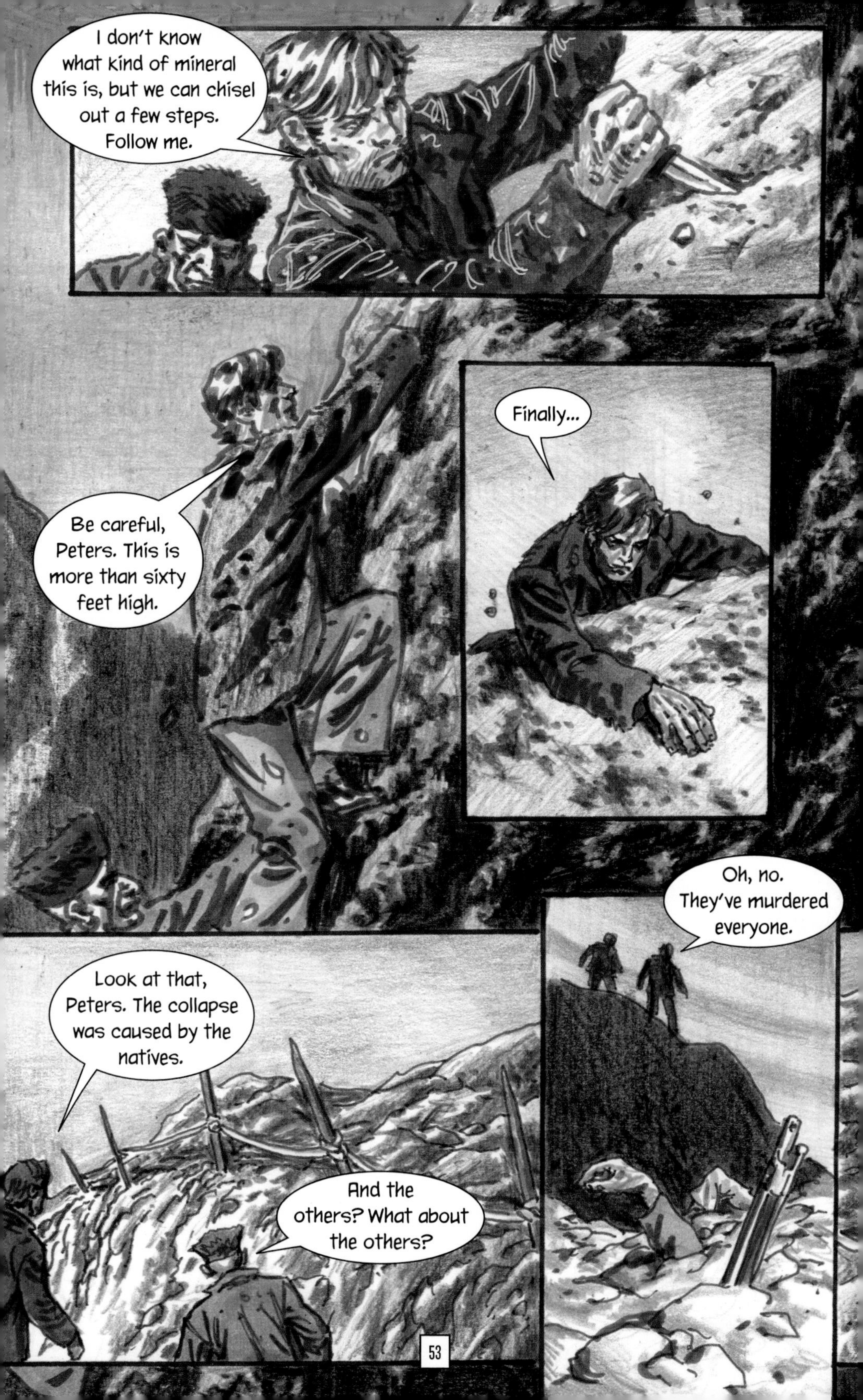
I don't know what kind of mineral this is, but we can chisel out a few steps. Follow me.
Be careful, Peters. This is more than sixty feet high.
Finally...
Oh, no. They've murdered everyone.
Look at that, Peters. The collapse was caused by the natives.
And the others? What about the others?

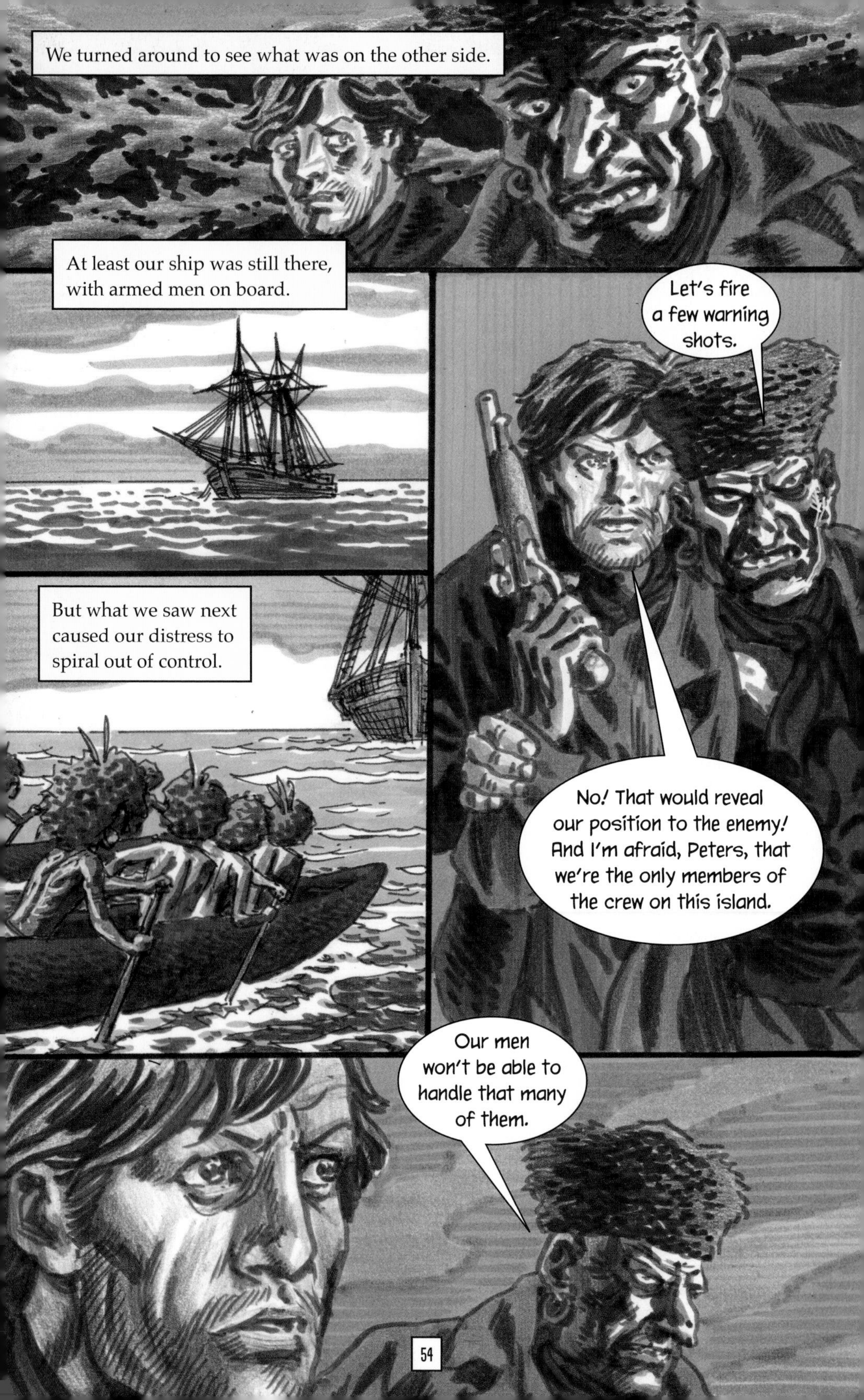

We turned around to see what was on the other side.
At least our ship was still there, with armed men on board.
Let's fire a few warning shots.
But what we saw next caused our distress to spiral out of control.
No! That would reveal our position to the enemy! And I'm afraid, Peters, that we're the only members of the crew on this island.
Our men won't be able to handle that many of them.

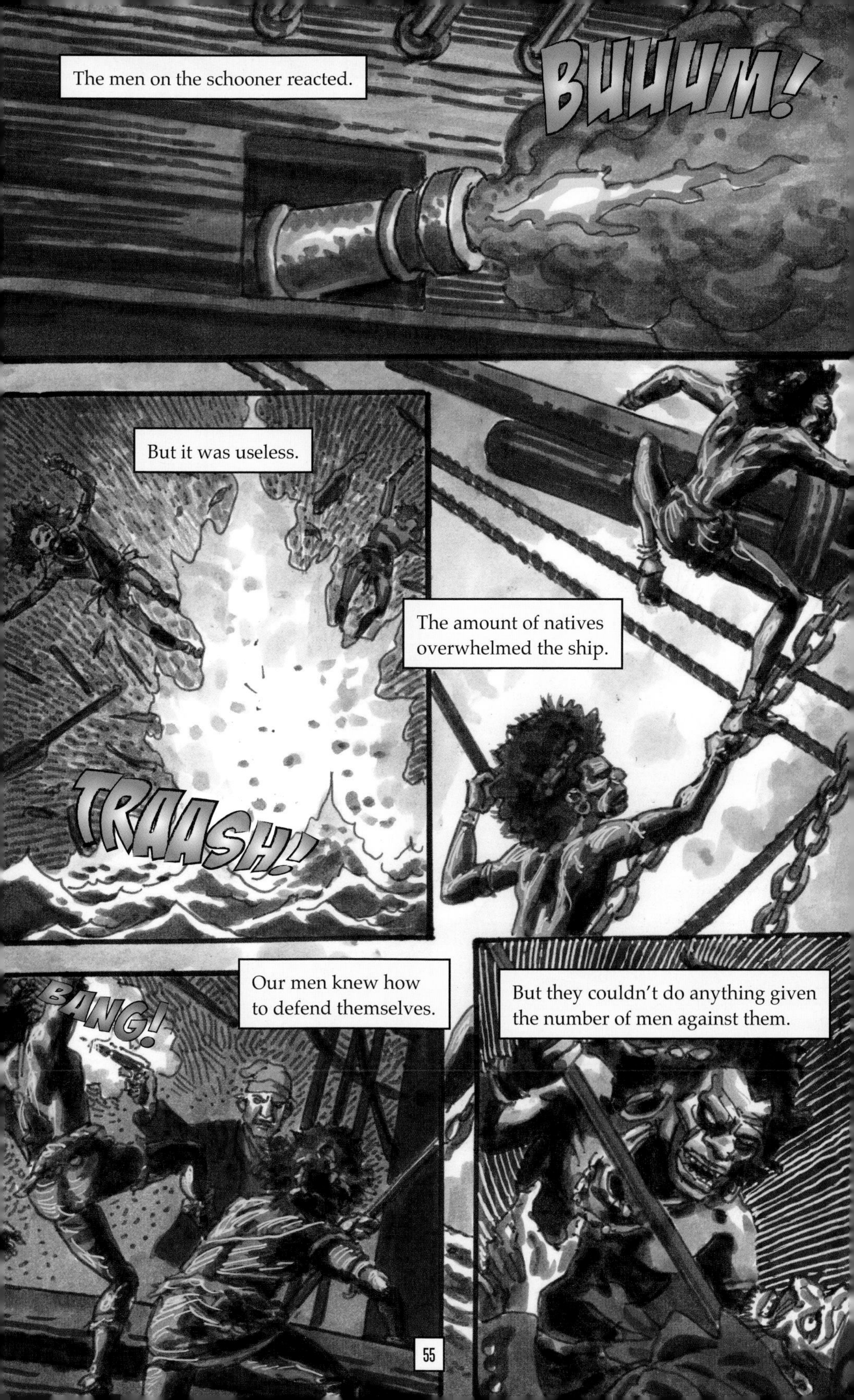

The men on the schooner reacted.
BUUUM!
But it was useless.
TRAAASH!
The amount of natives overwhelmed the ship.
BANG!
Our men knew how to defend themselves.
But they couldn't do anything given the number of men against them.

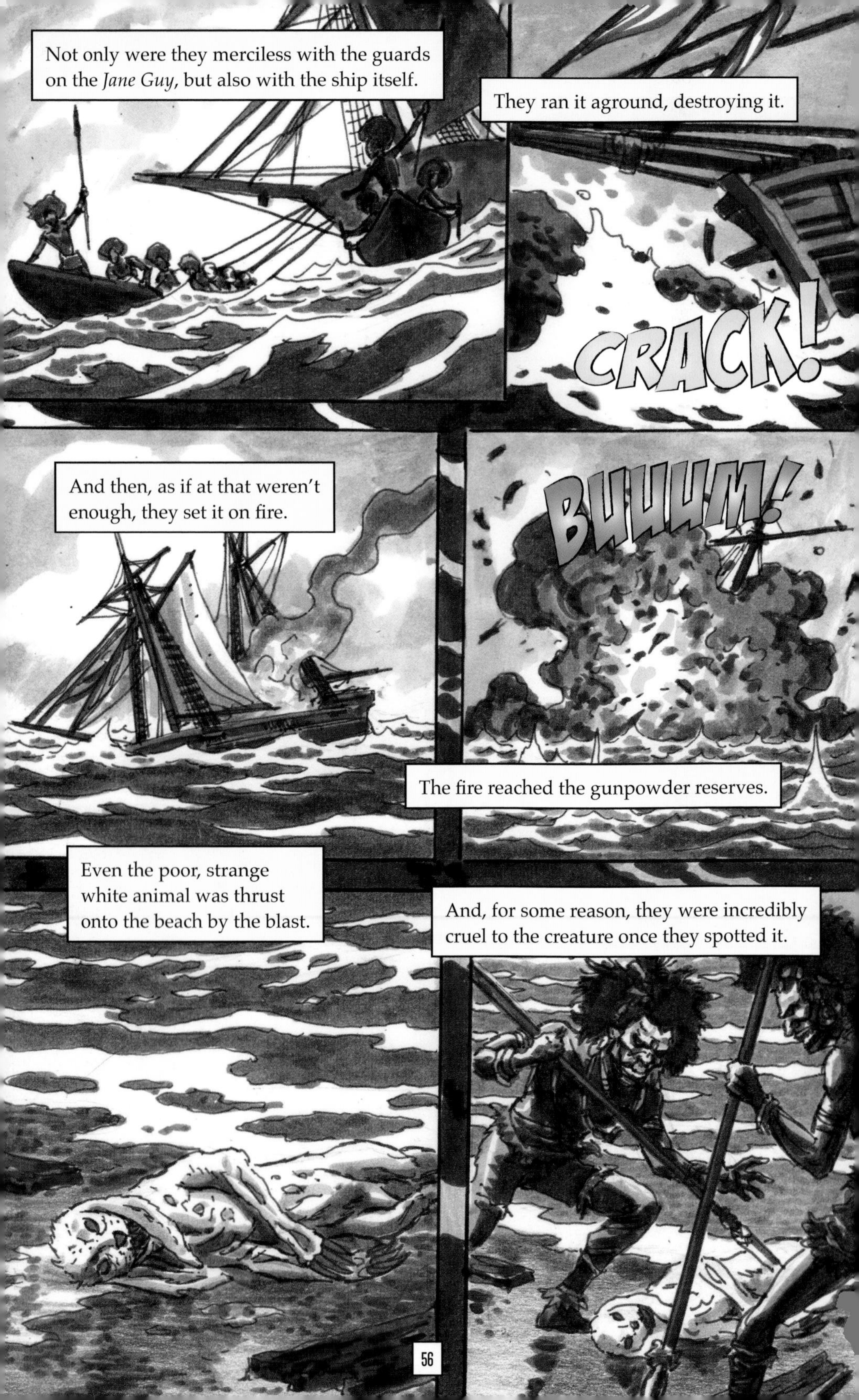
Not only were they merciless with the guards on the *Jane Guy*, but also with the ship itself.
They ran it aground, destroying it.
CRACK!
And then, as if at that weren't enough, they set it on fire.
BUUUM!
The fire reached the gunpowder reserves.
Even the poor, strange white animal was thrust onto the beach by the blast.
And, for some reason, they were incredibly cruel to the creature once they spotted it.

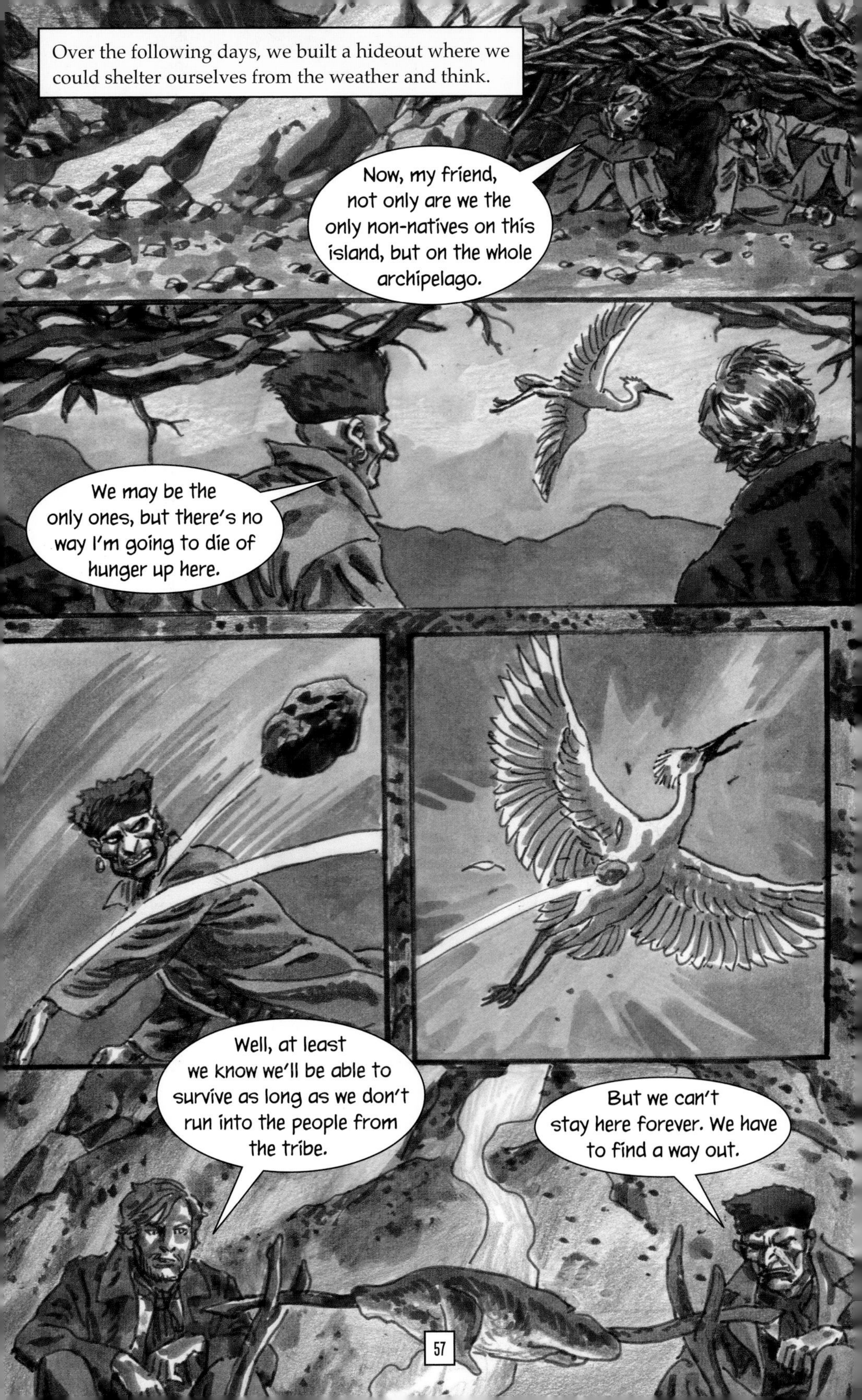

Over the following days, we built a hideout where we could shelter ourselves from the weather and think.
Now, my friend, not only are we the only non-natives on this island, but on the whole archipelago.
We may be the only ones, but there's no way I'm going to die of hunger up here.
Well, at least we know we'll be able to survive as long as we don't run into the people from the tribe.
But we can't stay here forever. We have to find a way out.

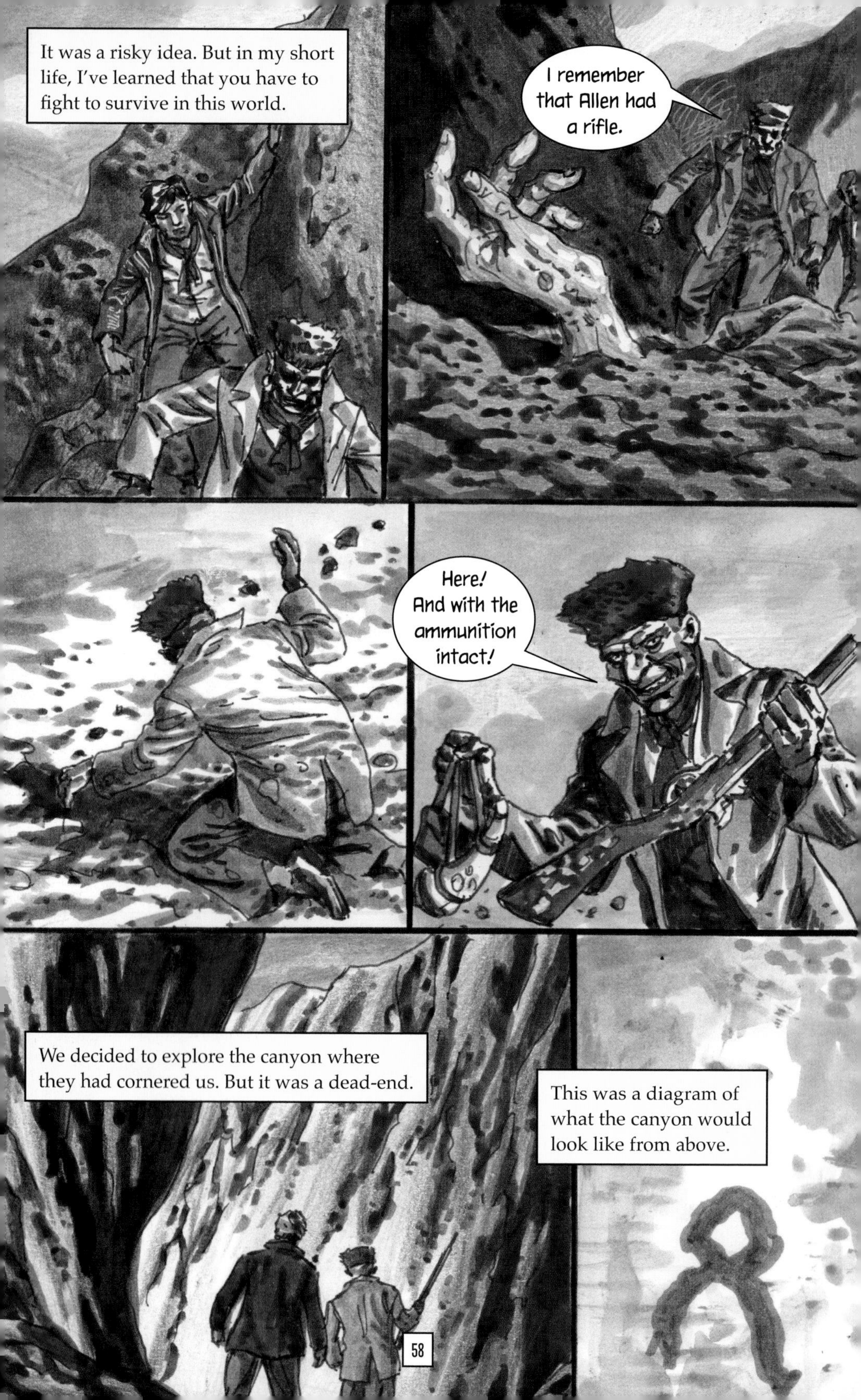
It was a risky idea. But in my short life, I've learned that you have to fight to survive in this world.
I remember that Allen had a rifle.
Here! And with the ammunition intact!
We decided to explore the canyon where they had cornered us. But it was a dead-end.
This was a diagram of what the canyon would look like from above.

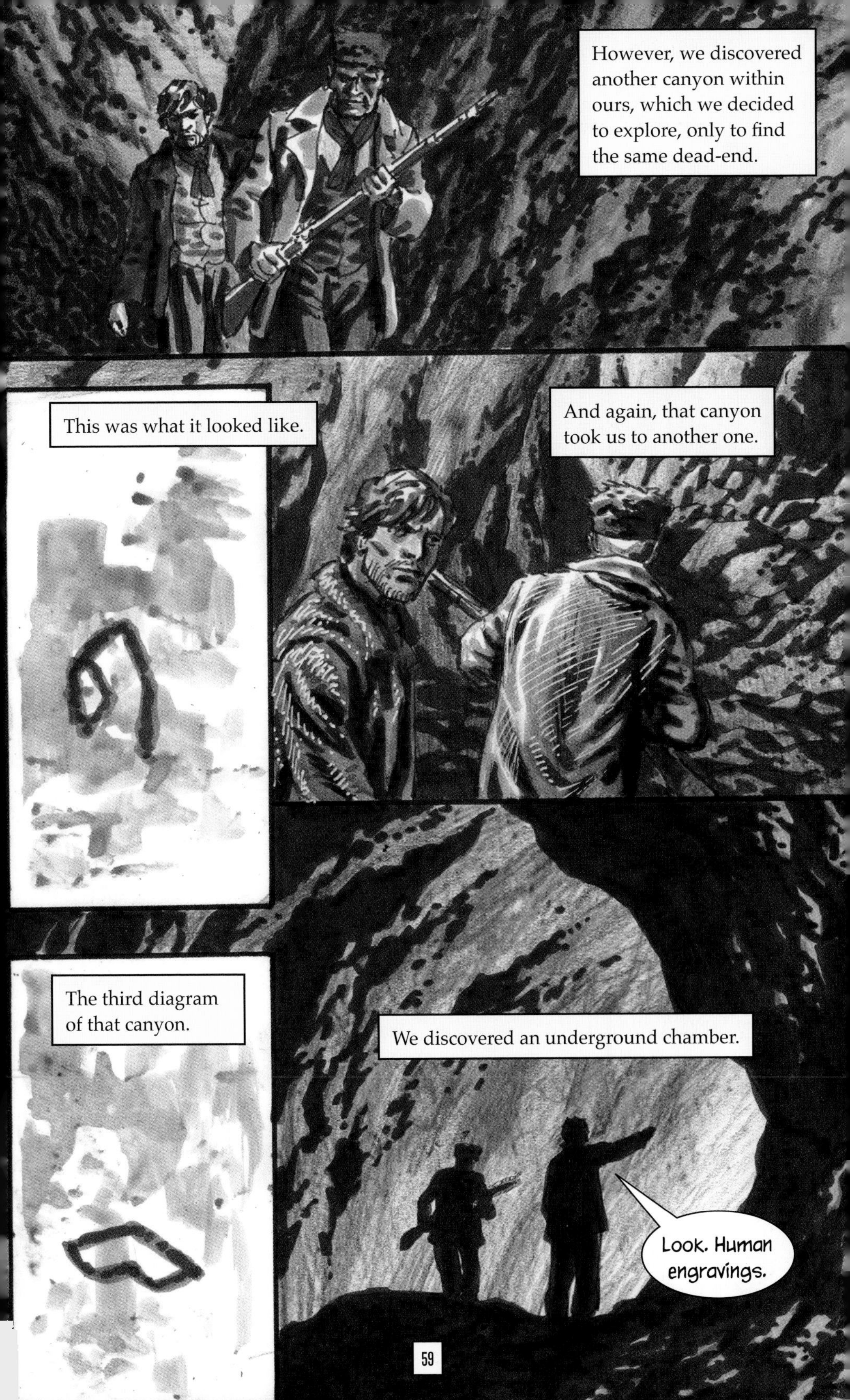
However, we discovered another canyon within ours, which we decided to explore, only to find the same dead-end.
This was what it looked like.
And again, that canyon took us to another one.
The third diagram of that canyon.
We discovered an underground chamber.
Look. Human engravings.

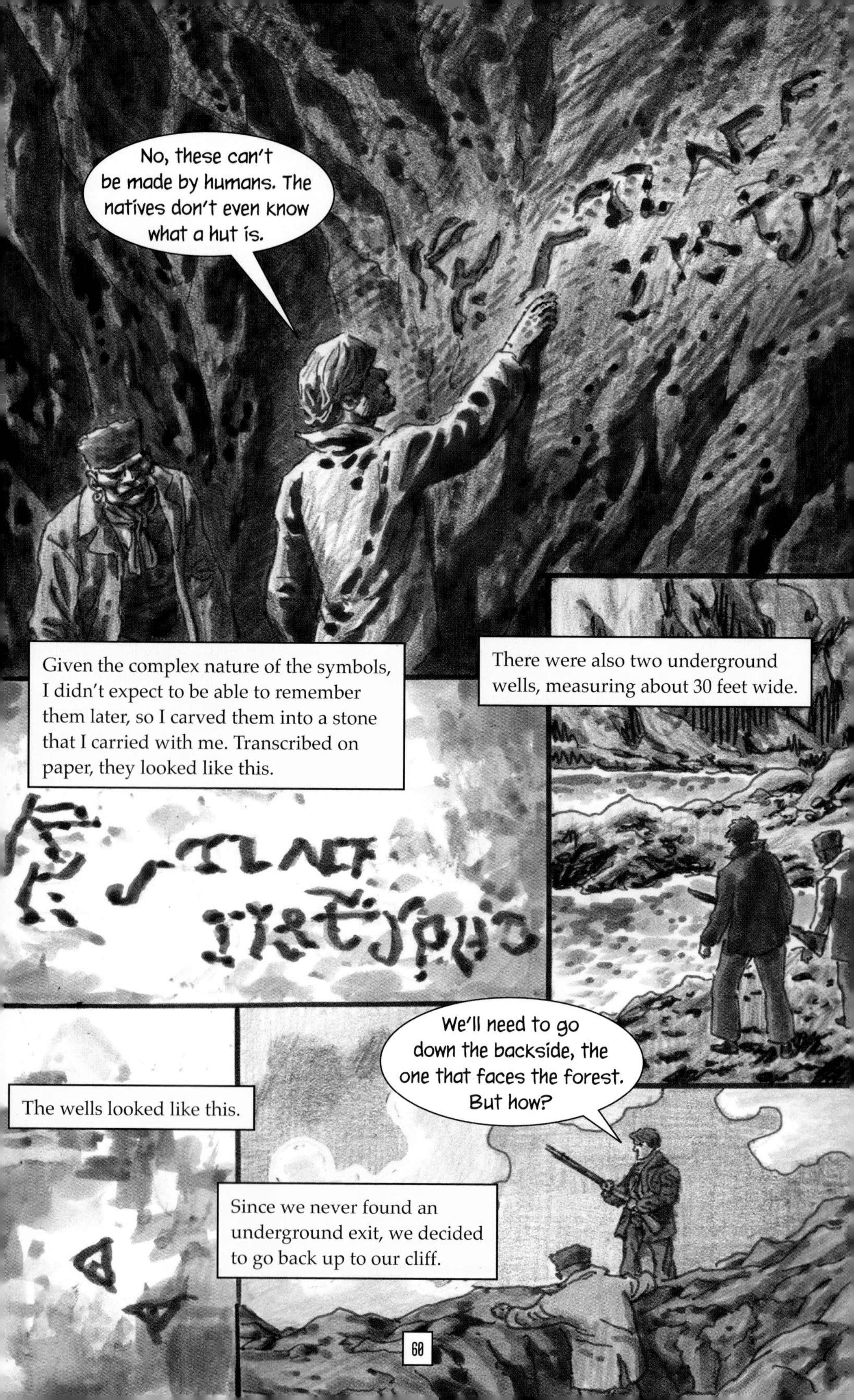

No, these can't be made by humans. The natives don't even know what a hut is.
Given the complex nature of the symbols, I didn't expect to be able to remember them later, so I carved them into a stone that I carried with me. Transcribed on paper, they looked like this.
There were also two underground wells, measuring about 30 feet wide.
The wells looked like this.
We'll need to go down the backside, the one that faces the forest. But how?
Since we never found an underground exit, we decided to go back up to our cliff.

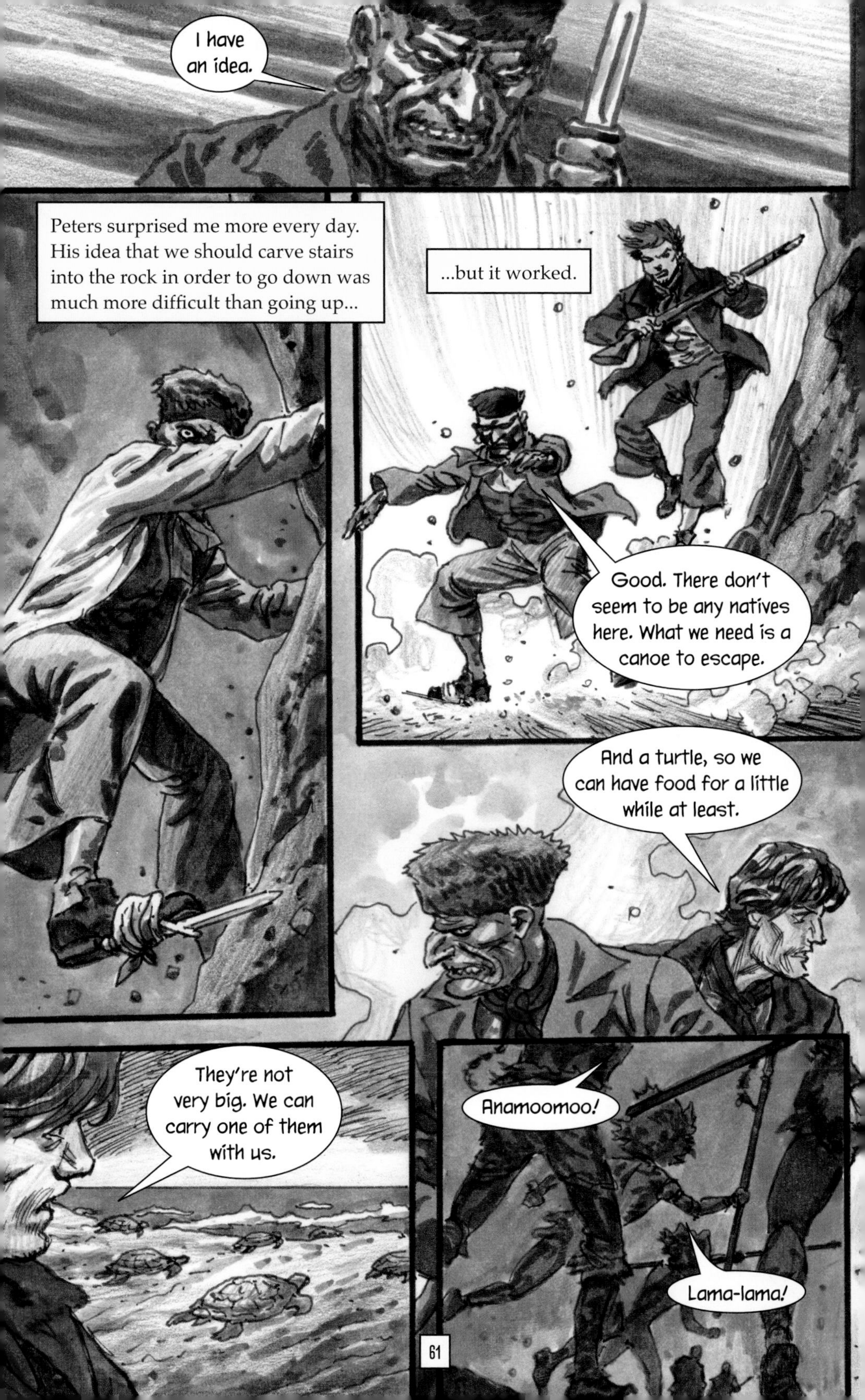
I have an idea.
Peters surprised me more every day. His idea that we should carve stairs into the rock in order to go down was much more difficult than going up...
...but it worked.
Good. There don't seem to be any natives here. What we need is a canoe to escape.
And a turtle, so we can have food for a little while at least.
They're not very big. We can carry one of them with us.
Anamoomoo!
Lama-lama!

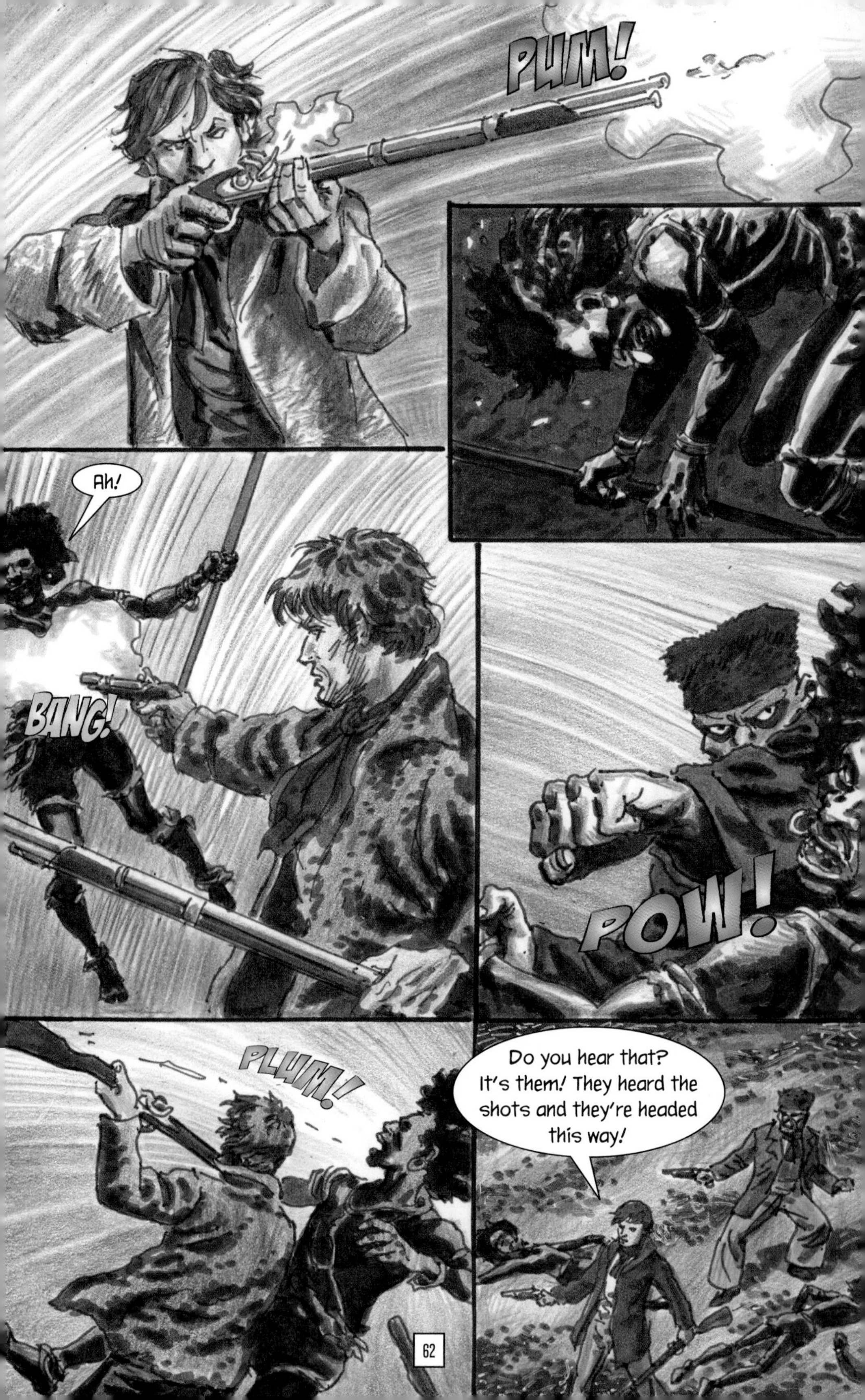
PUM!
Ah!
BANG!
POW!
PLUM!
Do you hear that? It's them! They heard the shots and they're headed this way!

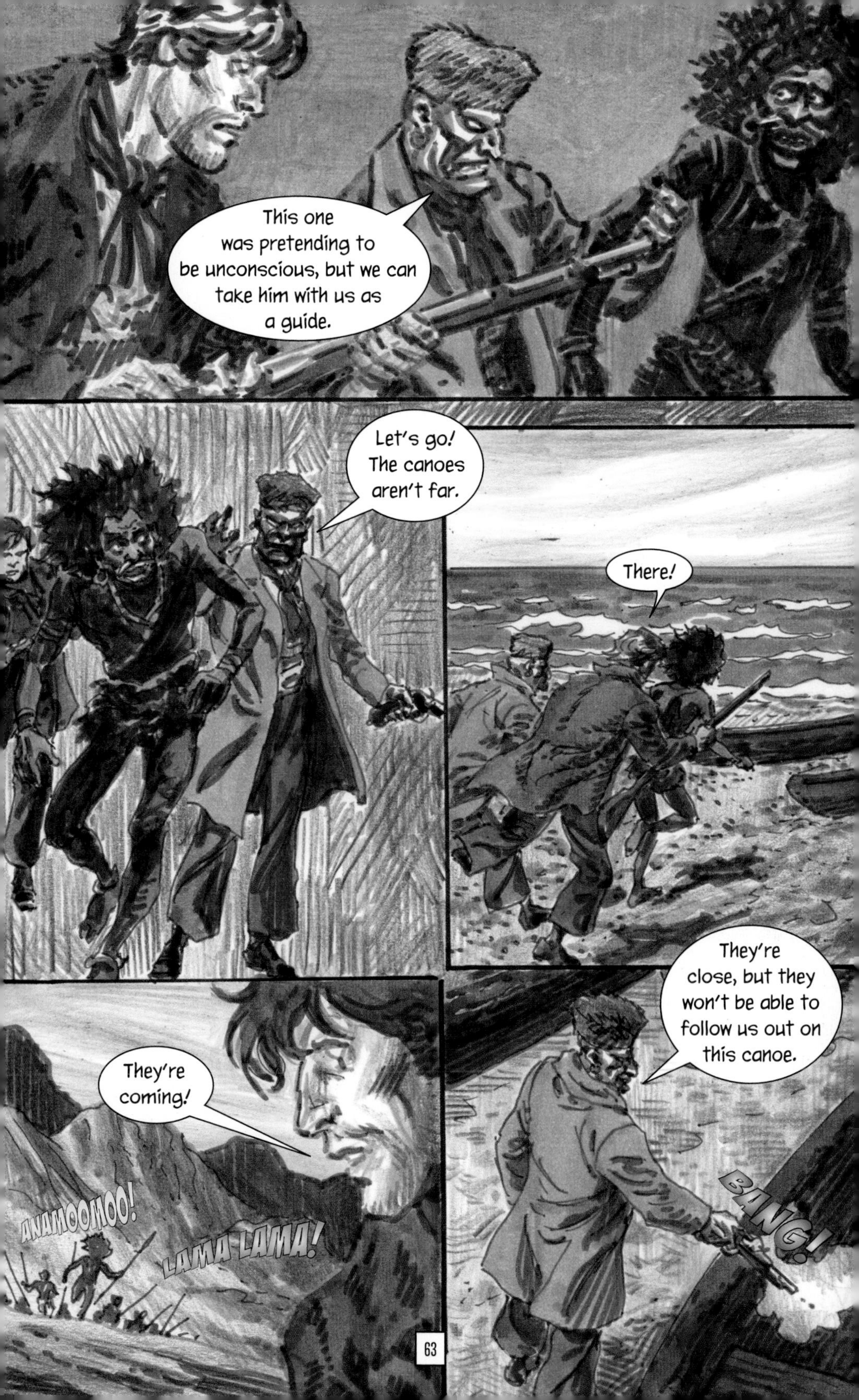

This one was pretending to be unconscious, but we can take him with us as a guide.
Let's go! The canoes aren't far.
There!
They're coming!
ANAMOOMOO!
LAMA LAMA!
They're close, but they won't be able to follow us out on this canoe.
BANG!

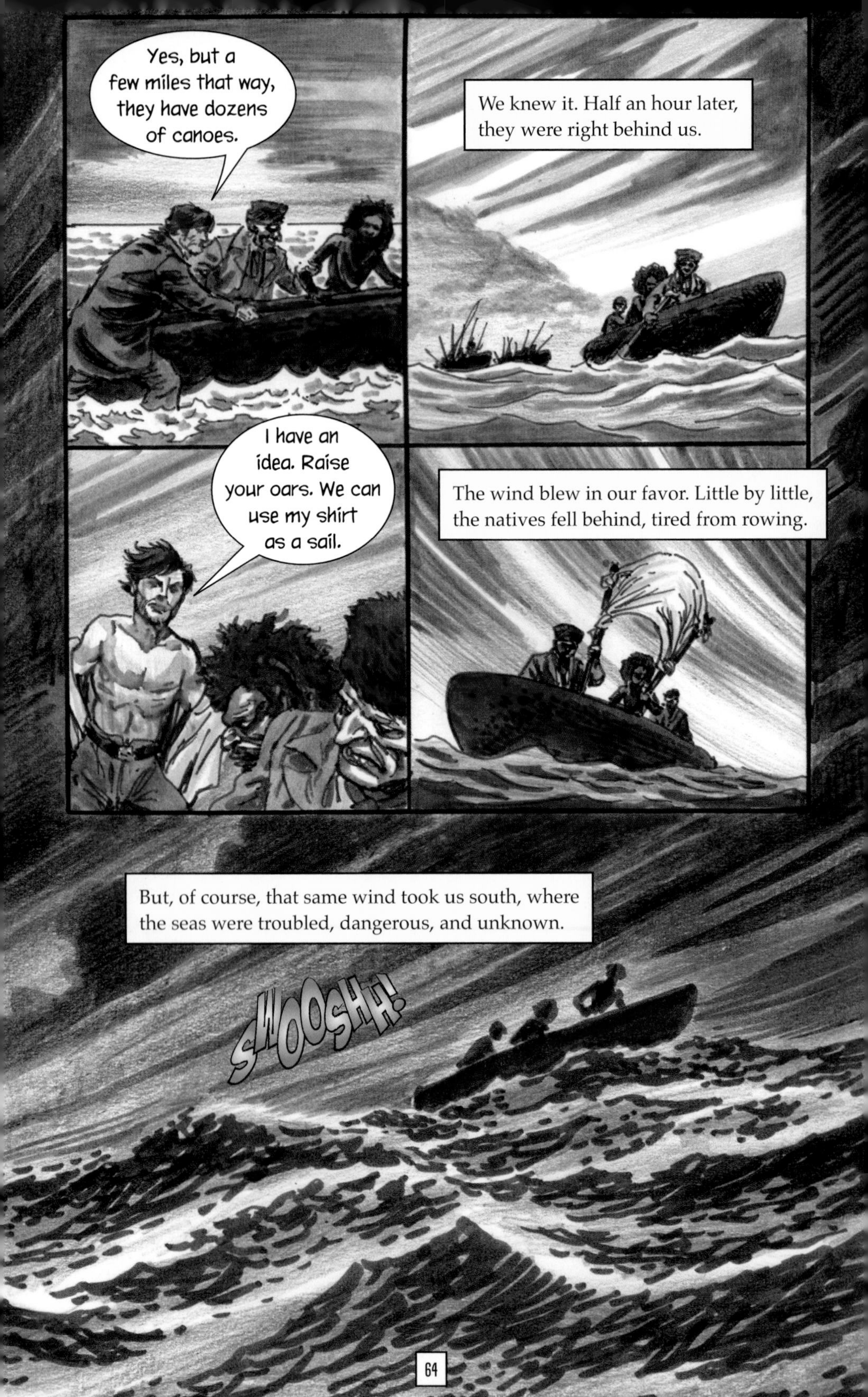
Yes, but a few miles that way, they have dozens of canoes.
We knew it. Half an hour later, they were right behind us.
I have an idea. Raise your oars. We can use my shirt as a sail.
The wind blew in our favor. Little by little, the natives fell behind, tired from rowing.
But, of course, that same wind took us south, where the seas were troubled, dangerous, and unknown.
SWOOSHH!

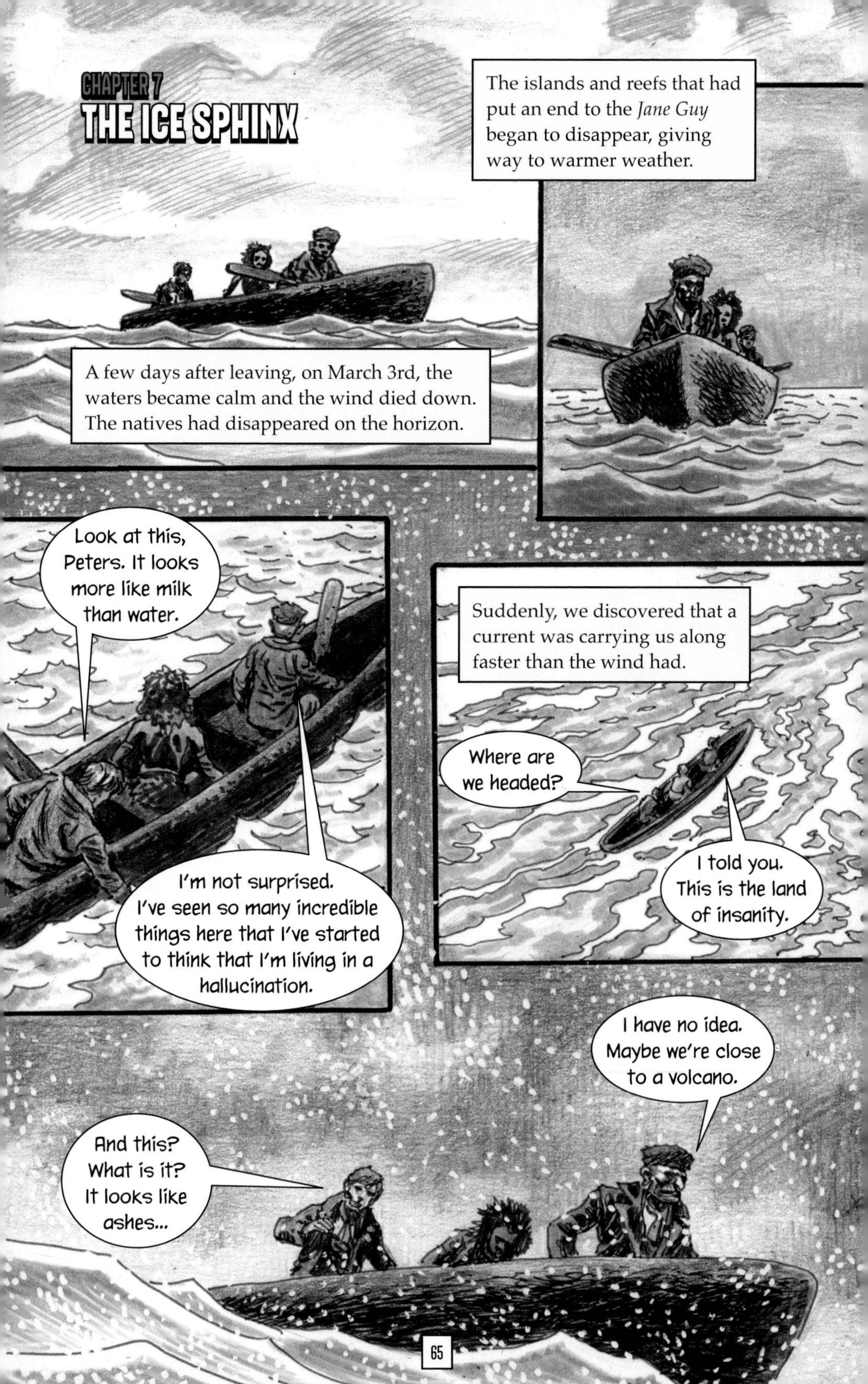
CHAPTER 7
THE ICE SPHINX
The islands and reefs that had put an end to the *Jane Guy* began to disappear, giving way to warmer weather.
A few days after leaving, on March 3rd, the waters became calm and the wind died down. The natives had disappeared on the horizon.
Look at this, Peters. It looks more like milk than water.
I'm not surprised. I've seen so many incredible things here that I've started to think that I'm living in a hallucination.
Suddenly, we discovered that a current was carrying us along faster than the wind had.
Where are we headed?
I told you. This is the land of insanity.
And this? What is it? It looks like ashes...
I have no idea. Maybe we're close to a volcano.

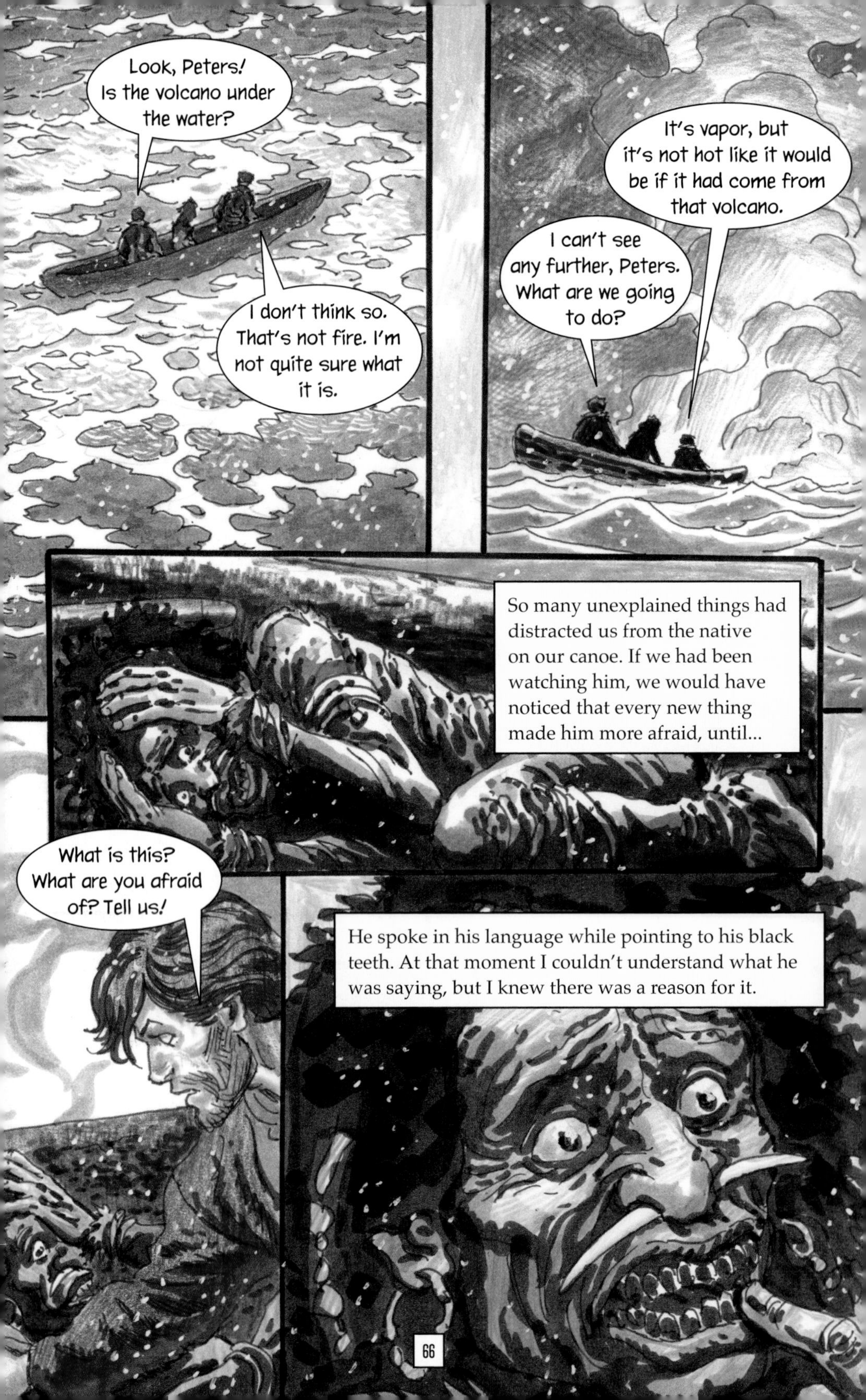

Look, Peters! Is the volcano under the water?
I don't think so. That's not fire. I'm not quite sure what it is.
I can't see any further, Peters. What are we going to do?
It's vapor, but it's not hot like it would be if it had come from that volcano.
So many unexplained things had distracted us from the native on our canoe. If we had been watching him, we would have noticed that every new thing made him more afraid, until...
What is this? What are you afraid of? Tell us!
He spoke in his language while pointing to his black teeth. At that moment I couldn't understand what he was saying, but I knew there was a reason for it.

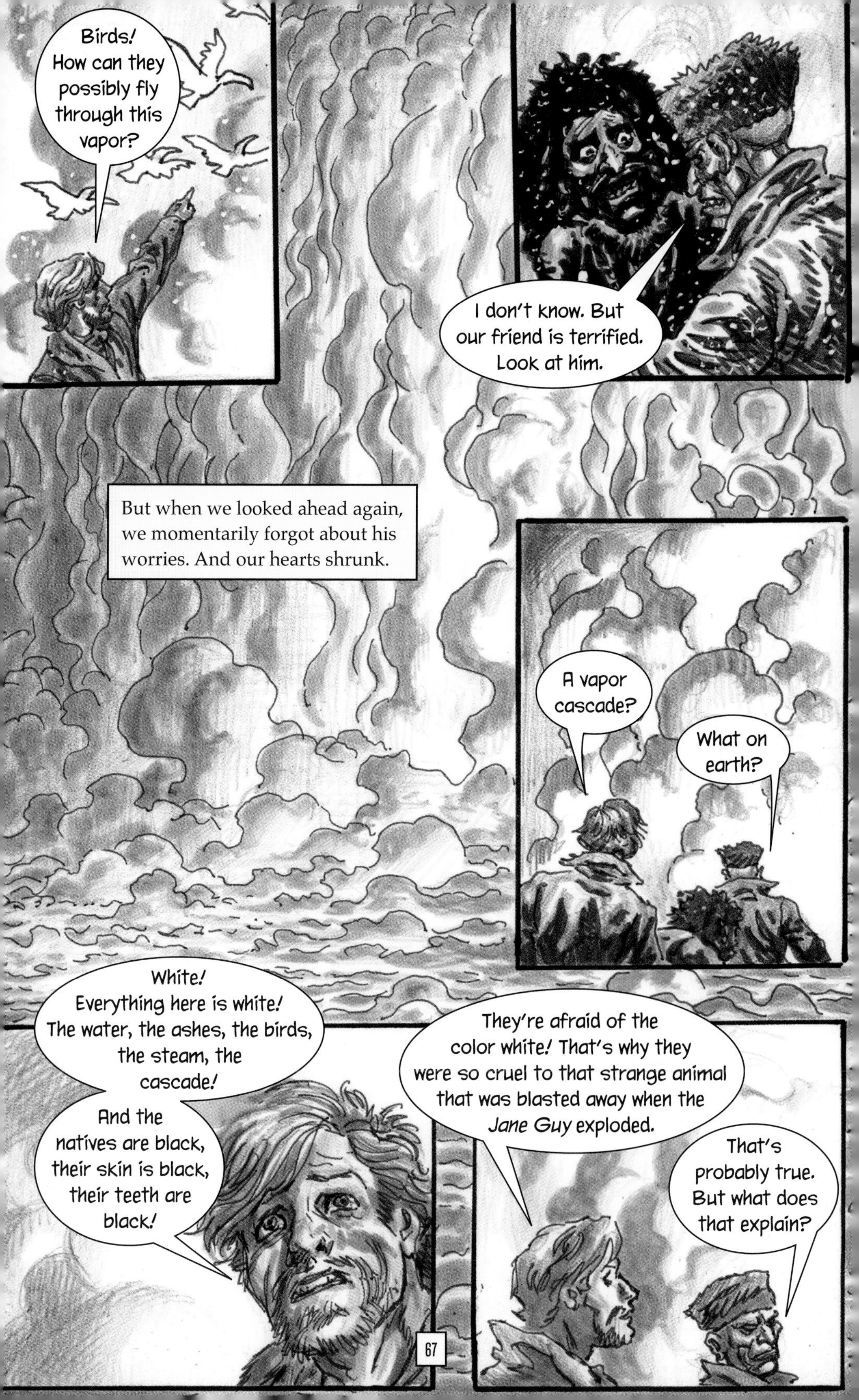
Birds! How can they possibly fly through this vapor?
I don't know. But our friend is terrified. Look at him.
But when we looked ahead again, we momentarily forgot about his worries. And our hearts shrunk.
A vapor cascade?
What on earth?
White! Everything here is white! The water, the ashes, the birds, the steam, the cascade!
And the natives are black, their skin is black, their teeth are black!
They're afraid of the color white! That's why they were so cruel to that strange animal that was blasted away when the *Jane Guy* exploded.
That's probably true. But what does that explain?

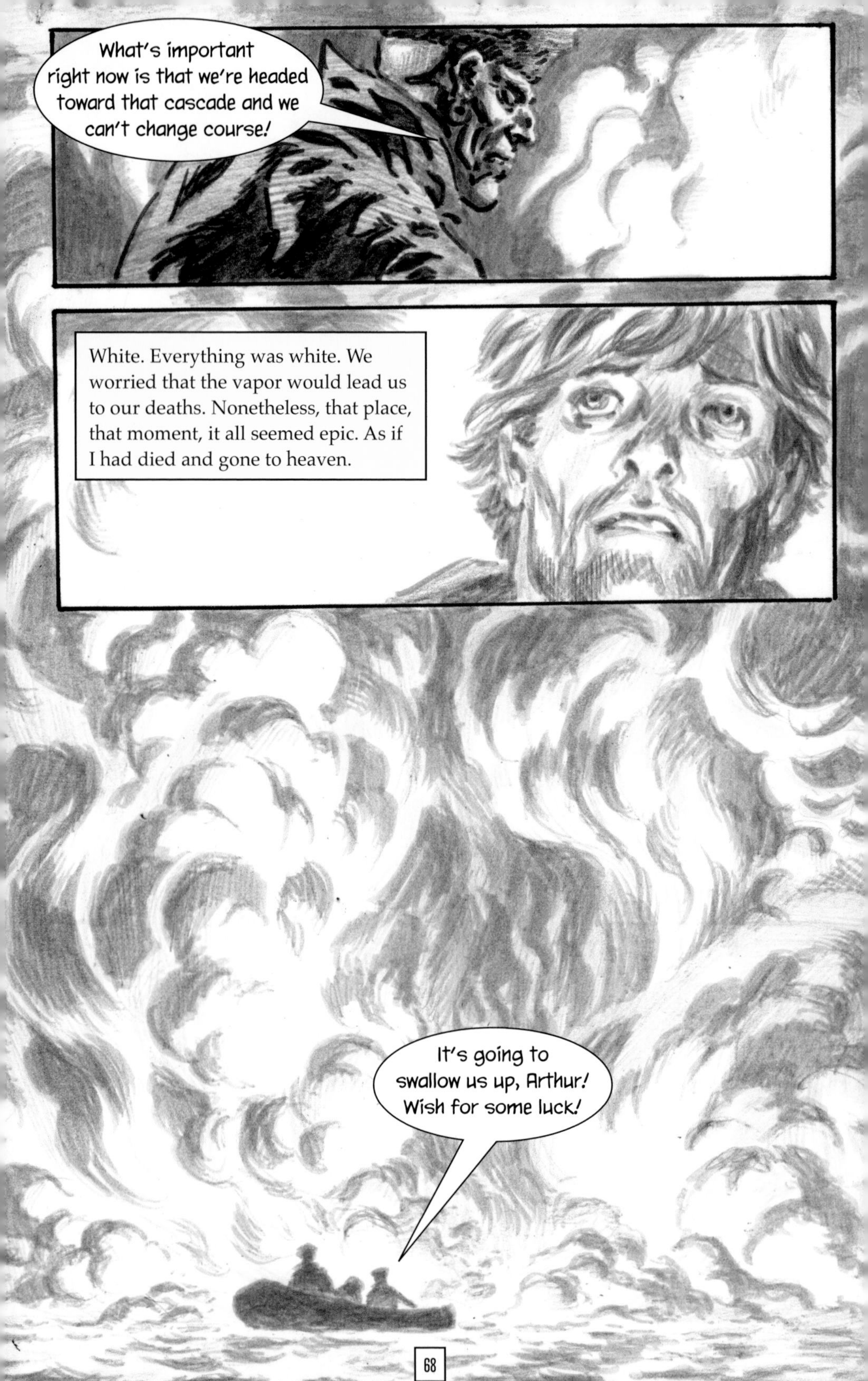

What's important right now is that we're headed toward that cascade and we can't change course!
White. Everything was white. We worried that the vapor would lead us to our deaths. Nonetheless, that place, that moment, it all seemed epic. As if I had died and gone to heaven.
It's going to swallow us up, Arthur! Wish for some luck!

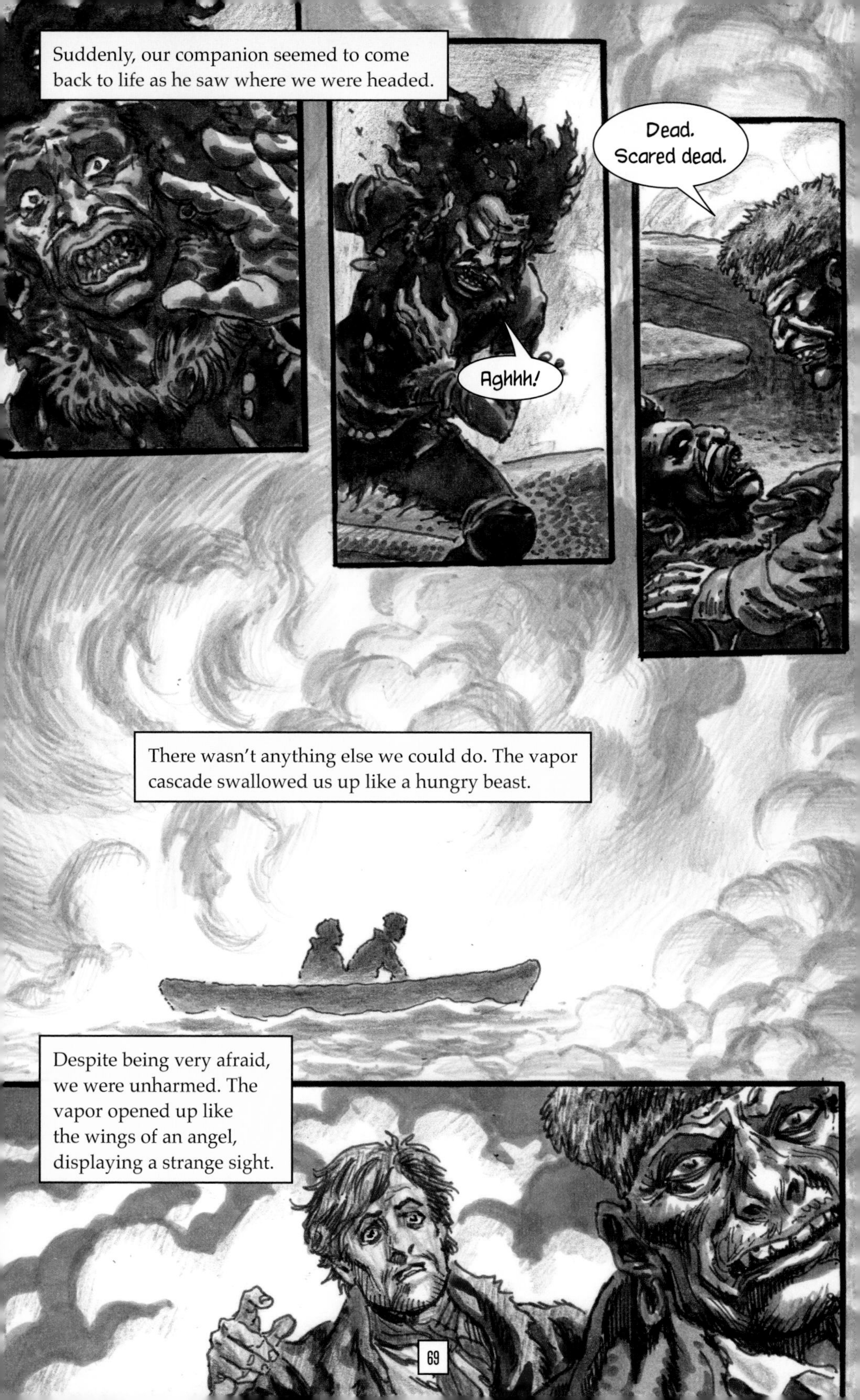

Suddenly, our companion seemed to come back to life as he saw where we were headed.
Aghhh!
Dead. Scared dead.
There wasn't anything else we could do. The vapor cascade swallowed us up like a hungry beast.
Despite being very afraid, we were unharmed. The vapor opened up like the wings of an angel, displaying a strange sight.

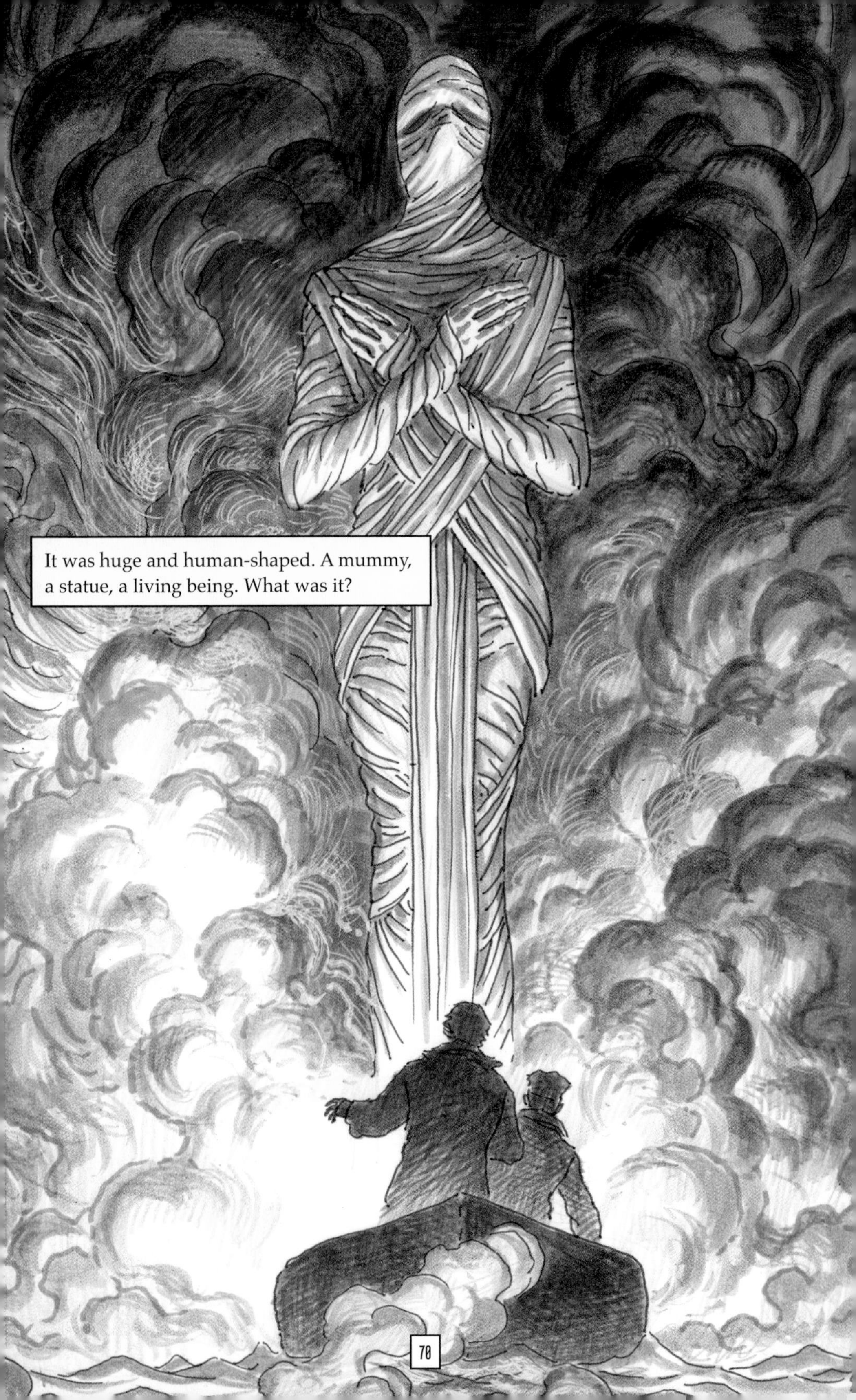
It was huge and human-shaped. A mummy, a statue, a living being. What was it?

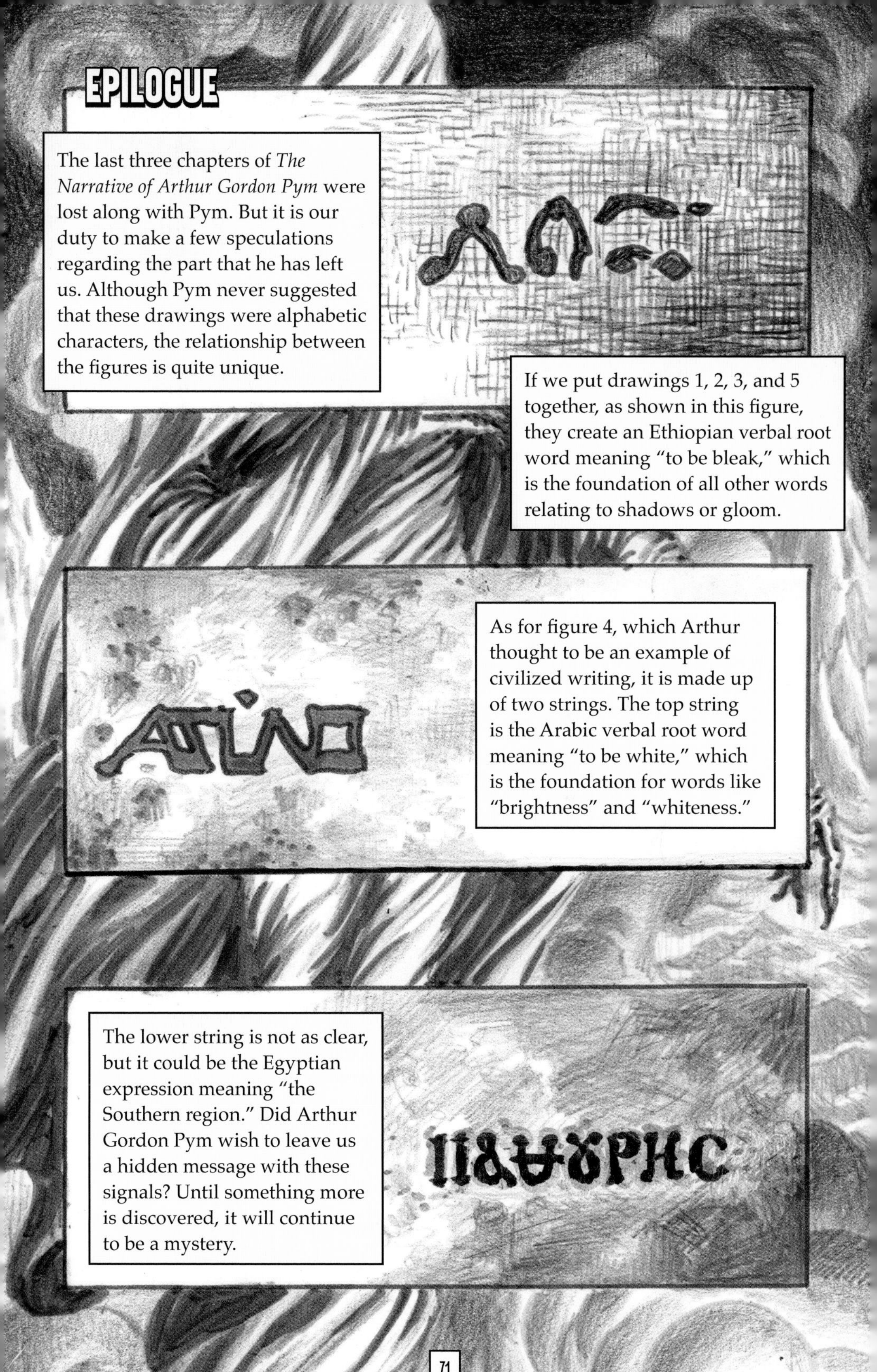
EPILOGUE
The last three chapters of *The Narrative of Arthur Gordon Pym* were lost along with Pym. But it is our duty to make a few speculations regarding the part that he has left us. Although Pym never suggested that these drawings were alphabetic characters, the relationship between the figures is quite unique.
If we put drawings 1, 2, 3, and 5 together, as shown in this figure, they create an Ethiopian verbal root word meaning "to be bleak," which is the foundation of all other words relating to shadows or gloom.
As for figure 4, which Arthur thought to be an example of civilized writing, it is made up of two strings. The top string is the Arabic verbal root word meaning "to be white," which is the foundation for words like "brightness" and "whiteness."
The lower string is not as clear, but it could be the Egyptian expression meaning "the Southern region." Did Arthur Gordon Pym wish to leave us a hidden message with these signals? Until something more is discovered, it will continue to be a mystery.

ABOUT THE AUTHOR

Edgar Allan Poe was born in Boston, Massachusetts, in 1809. His biological parents, the Poes, died when he was a child, and he was taken in by the Allans, thus giving him his first last name. He published his first book of poems in 1827, but due to economic troubles, he would soon focus his literary efforts on writing short stories and brief literary and art criticism reviews. In 1845, he published a poem titled "The Raven," which would provide him great fame, but not a lot of money. He died in 1849. He was 40 years old. The circumstances of his death are quite mysterious, and the true cause is still a topic of debate. Despite his early death, the influence of his works on writers around the world became apparent, both on his peers, such as Charles Baudelaire, Jules Verne, and Fyodor Dostoyevski, and later writers, such as H.P. Lovecraft and Stephen King.

ABOUT THE RETELLING AUTHOR AND ILLUSTRATOR

Manuel Morini studied film at the Superior School of Cinematography in Argentina. He took several seminars on scripts. He created and wrote the script for two comics, *Khrysé* and *Crazy Jack*. He was a screenwriter for *Nippur de Lagash*, *Savarese*, and *Dago*. In 1993, he won the comic of the year prize, presented by the Magazine Editors Association. He is currently a screenwriting professor at the "Sótano Blanco" school, and is a consultant at Bureau de Guionistas.

Enrique Alcatena, from Buenos Aires, Argentina, is a comic strip cartoonist, illustrator, and screenwriter. His works tend to be categorized in the genre of fantasy. They have been published not only in his country, but also in North America, Europe, and Asia.

GLOSSARY

archipelago (ar-kuh-PE-luh-goh)—a group of islands

barnacle (BAR-ni-kuhl)—a small shellfish that attaches itself to the side of a ship

brig (BRIGG)—where prisoners are held on a ship

drowsiness (DROW-see-nehss)—feeling of being ready to fall asleep

eroding (i-ROH-ding)—the wearing away of land by water or wind

mutineers (MYOOT-uh-neers)—crew members who revolt against a captain of a ship

spirit (SPIHR-it)—alcohol

starboard (STAR-burd)—right-hand side of a ship

stowaway (stow-uh-WAY)—a person who hides on a ship for free passage

THE MYSTERIES OF THE SOUTH POLE

For centuries, the most southern region on Earth was completely unknown. Its mysteries were revealed a little more than a century ago, meaning that Antarctica was long the object of assumptions and myths that only the bravest explorers dared to face.

Even so far back as ancient Greece, scientific thinkers guessed that, given Earth's round shape, there must have been a landmass in the Southern Hemisphere big enough to act as a counterweight to that existing in the Northern Hemisphere. Thus, Claudius Ptolemy was the first person to depict this continent on a world map, which he named *Terra Australis Incognita*. At that point in time, it was assumed to be a continuation of the African continent.

This hypothetical continent continued to appear on world maps with this name, even after North and South America were discovered. In 1520, when Ferdinand Magellan discovered a strait at the very southern tip of the American continent, he spotted the archipelago Tierra del Fuego and believed that a continent called *Terra Australis* began there. A few years later, a Spanish expedition passing through the Strait of Magellan was forced south of their route. It became the first one to sail beyond Cape Horn, where Tierra del Fuego ends, and proved that this was not, in fact, part of *Terra Australis*. From that moment, this name was reserved for the country we now know as Australia. In the early sixteenth century, the first sightings were made of what was truly Antarctica, although people continued to have the primitive idea that it was a huge landmass, much larger than its actual size.

The first seafarer who decided to go explore Antarctica was James Cook. Up until his 1772 expedition, all the ships that had traveled that far south had been forced out of their original routes by strong wind currents. The expedition captained by Cook was the first one to voluntarily cross the 60th parallel south, where the Antarctic Circle begins. Cook traveled around the world, staying close to that parallel. He demonstrated that Antarctica was not attached to any of the known landmasses at that time.

Intensive exploration of Antarctica began in the 19th century. The first expeditions to spot the continent came from different places, and took place from 1820 to 1823. The first documented landing didn't occur until 1853. Up until the early 20th century, expeditions were limited to making zoological collections and observations about magnetism. In 1907, the first expedition that would go further into the continent began, headed by Irish explorer Ernest Shackleton. His goal was to conquer the South Pole, but this would happen just four years later, carried out by Norwegian Roal Amundsen's expedition. In a memorable race to achieve this goal, in which he competed with a British expedition, Amundsen managed to arrive at the South Pole on December 14, 1911. The British expedition arrived just one month later.

This obsession with discovering every corner of Earth and its mysteries was not just expressed by scientists and explorers. The rest of the world also held an interest in its mysteries. Edgar Allan Poe only wrote one novel in his whole life, *The Narrative of Arthur Gordon Pym* (1838). In it, the main character drifts through the mysteries of the southern end of the planet. The great adventure writer Jules Verne continued Poe's story in his novel *The Ice Sphinx* (1897), but unlike Poe, Verne leans toward scientific theories about magnetism. In the 20th century, H.P. Lovecraft revisited the topic in his novel about exploration and cosmic terror: *At the Mountains of Madness* (1936).

DISCUSSION
QUESTIONS

1. Why do you think that Arthur decided to join his friend Augustus on the adventure?

2. Why do you think Dirk Peters saved Augustus' life? What would you have done in his place?

3. In many of his stories, such as "The Pit and the Pendulum," "The Premature Burial," and "The Cask of Amontillado," Poe describes the fear of being buried alive. Do you think that this novel reflects that fear? At what point in the story?

4. Why do you think the natives of Antarctica were afraid of the color white? What do you think the figure that appears at the end of the story is?

WRITING
PROMPTS

1. This story is narrated from Arthur Gordon Pym's perspective. Choose one of the other characters and narrate the story from his point of view.

2. What do you think happened to the captain of the *Grampus*, Augustus' father, after the mutineers set him adrift?

3. The story of Arthur Gordon Pym has an open ending. Continue the story with what could have happened after they discovered the white figure.

4. Before dressing up as a ghost, Arthur mentions that there are lots of stories about phantoms, which are common on ships. Write a scary story including ghosts that takes place aboard a ship.

EDGAR ALLAN POE AND THE MOVIES

The Narrative of Arthur Gordon Pym was never turned into a movie, but many of Edgar Allan Poe's stories were adapted for the big screen from the very beginnings of film. Some stories made in the era of silent films include "The Pit and the Pendulum," "William Wilson," "The Murders in the Rue Morgue," and his famous poem, "The Raven."

The most memorable adaptations of works by Poe, however, are those carried out in the 1960s by director Roger Corman, featuring the unforgettable Vincent Price. From 1960 to 1964, this pair carried out adaptations of "The Fall of the House of Usher," "The Pit and the Pendulum," "The Black Cat," "The Facts in the Case of M. Valdemar," "The Raven," and "The Masque of the Red Death." Most of these adaptations were very liberal versions, some only slightly inspired by Poe's texts. Nonetheless, Vincent Price went down in history as a master of horror thanks to the characters he played.

The cartoon series *The Simpsons* also paid tribute to the fame of Edgar Allan Poe. One of their classic Halloween episodes features a humorous adaptation of "The Raven."

Edgar Allan Poe not only inspired the film industry with his stories, but some producers even decided to use him as a character. The 2012 movie *The Raven* features Poe helping the police track down a killer who is inspired by his writings.

READ THEM ALL!

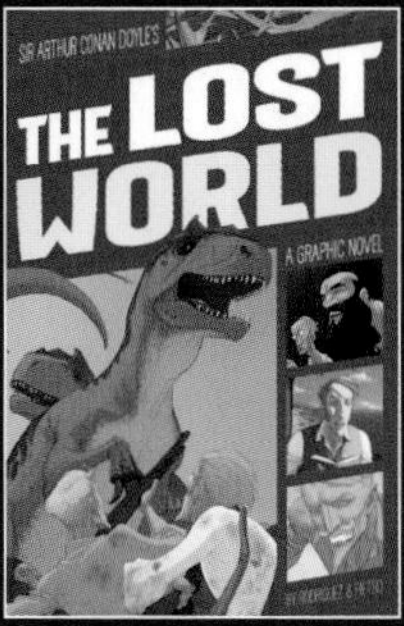

SIR ARTHUR CONAN DOYLE'S
THE LOST WORLD
A GRAPHIC NOVEL

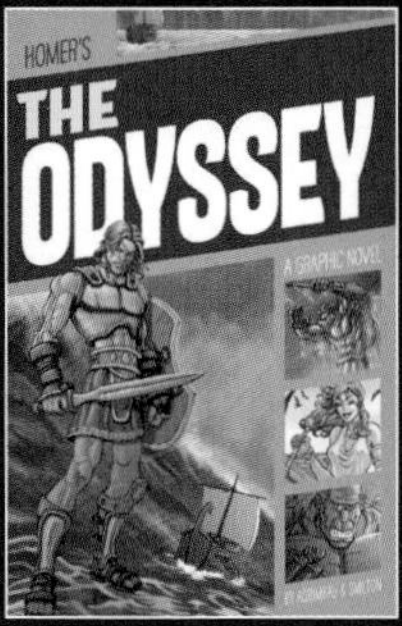

HOMER'S
THE ODYSSEY
A GRAPHIC NOVEL

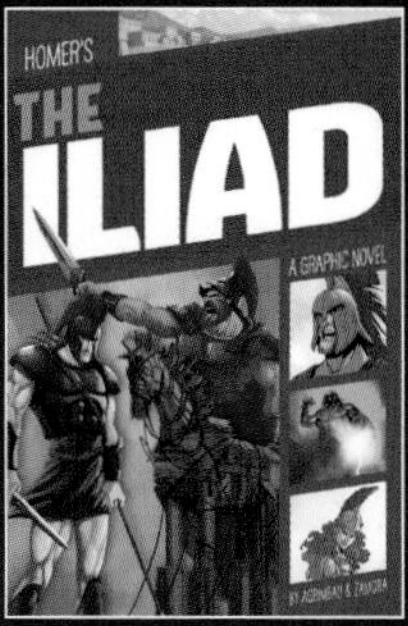

HOMER'S
THE ILIAD
A GRAPHIC NOVEL

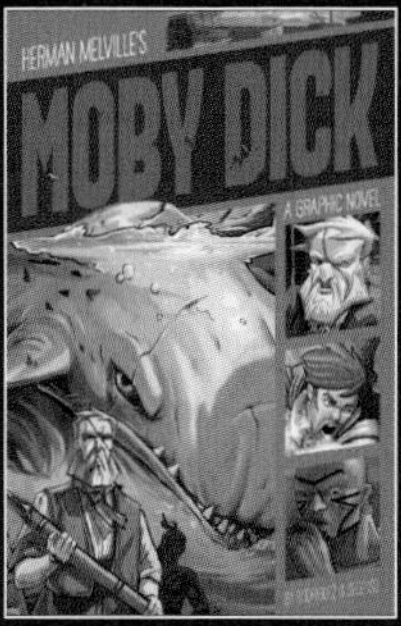

HERMAN MELVILLE'S
MOBY DICK
A GRAPHIC NOVEL

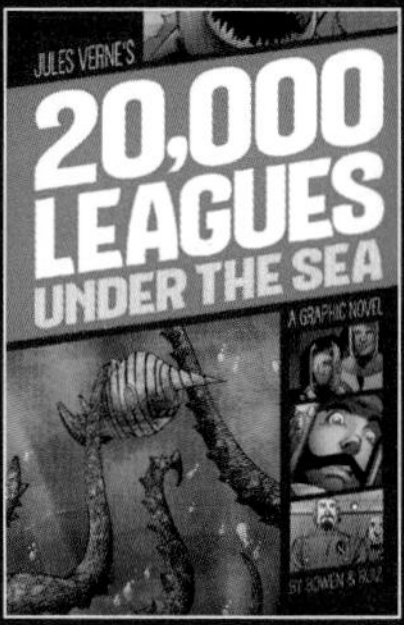

JULES VERNE'S
20,000 LEAGUES UNDER THE SEA
A GRAPHIC NOVEL

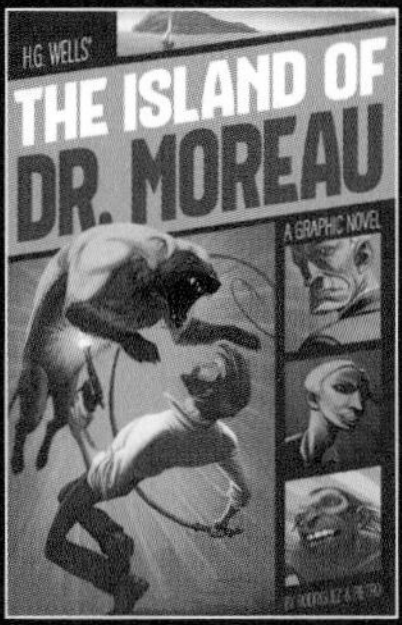

H.G. WELLS'
THE ISLAND OF DR. MOREAU
A GRAPHIC NOVEL

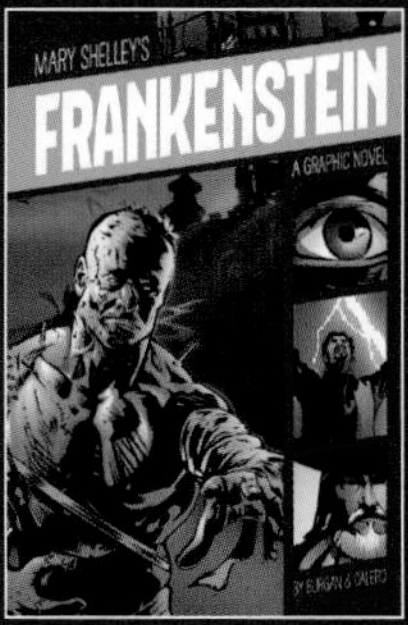

MARY SHELLEY'S
FRANKENSTEIN
A GRAPHIC NOVEL

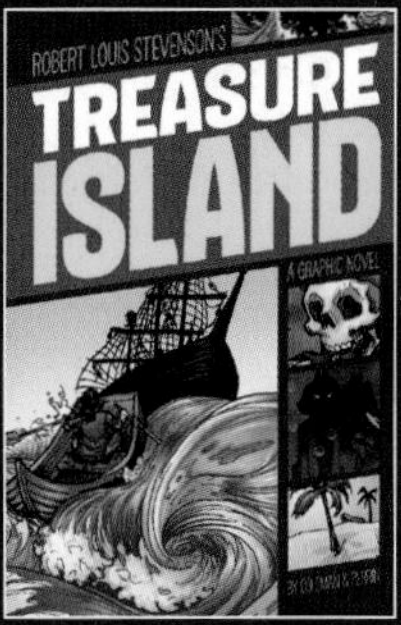

ROBERT LOUIS STEVENSON'S
TREASURE ISLAND
A GRAPHIC NOVEL

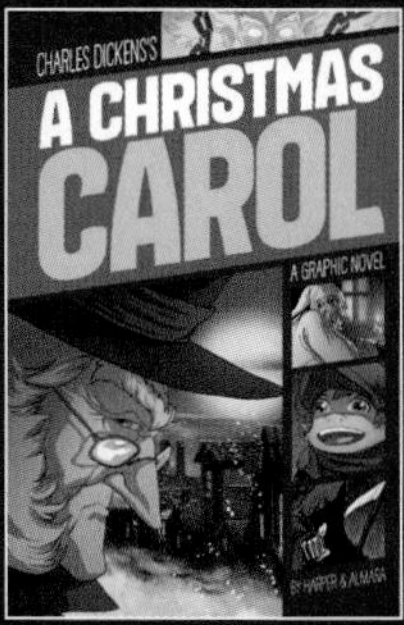

CHARLES DICKENS'S
A CHRISTMAS CAROL
A GRAPHIC NOVEL

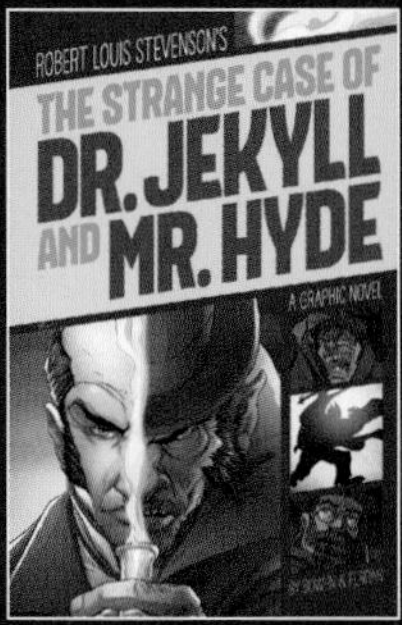

ROBERT LOUIS STEVENSON'S
THE STRANGE CASE OF DR. JEKYLL AND MR. HYDE
A GRAPHIC NOVEL

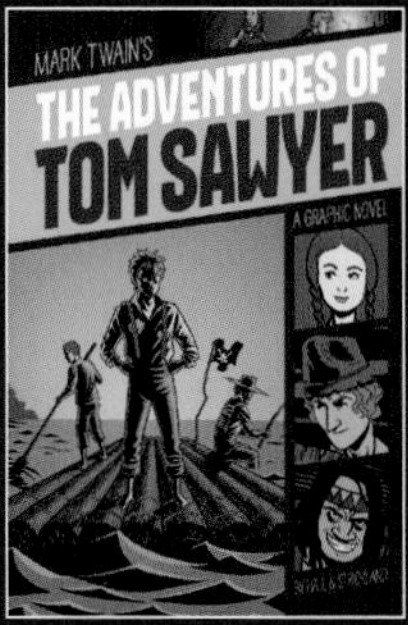

MARK TWAIN'S
THE ADVENTURES OF TOM SAWYER
A GRAPHIC NOVEL

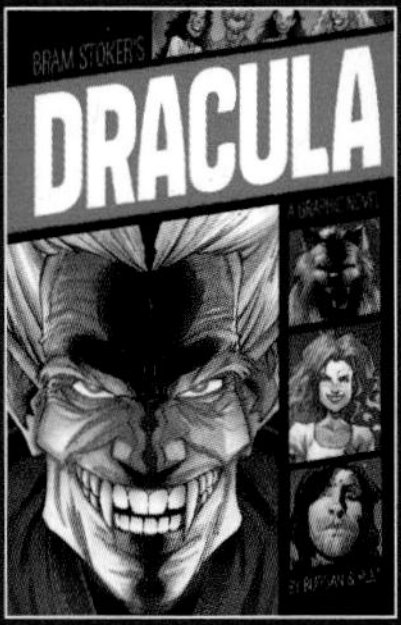

BRAM STOKER'S
DRACULA

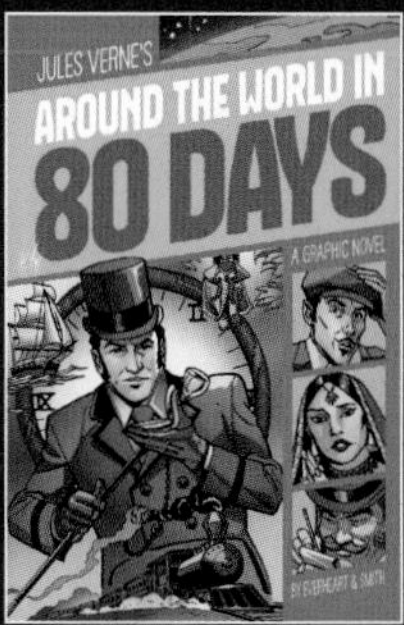

JULES VERNE'S
AROUND THE WORLD IN 80 DAYS
A GRAPHIC NOVEL

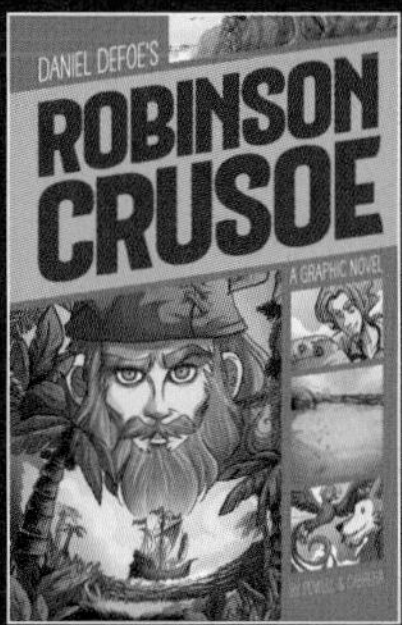

DANIEL DEFOE'S
ROBINSON CRUSOE
A GRAPHIC NOVEL

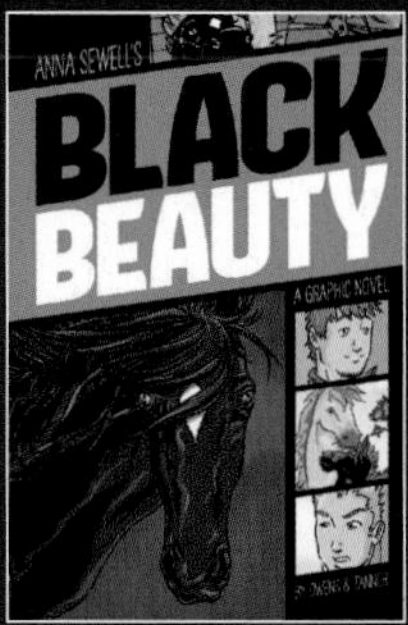

ANNA SEWELL'S
BLACK BEAUTY
A GRAPHIC NOVEL

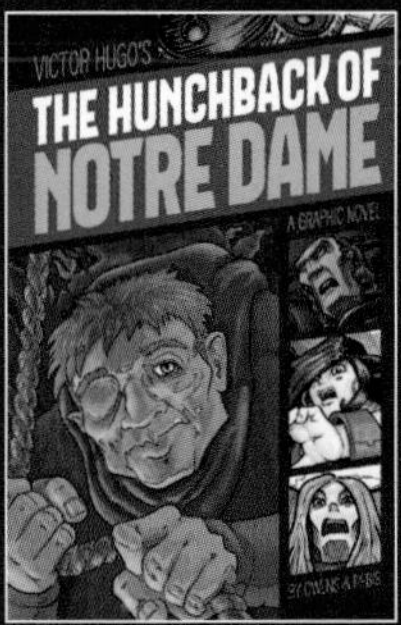

VICTOR HUGO'S
THE HUNCHBACK OF NOTRE DAME
A GRAPHIC NOVEL

ONLY FROM STONE ARCH BOOKS!